WHAT WILL HAPPEN IN

eragon
IV

"Richard Marcus brings refreshing intelligence, creativity and insight to his writing. He never disappoints."

James Barclay, author of *The Chronicles of The Raven* and *The Legend of The Raven*

"What Will Happen in Eragon IV reads like a conversation among well-informed Paolini fans; Marcus leaves few questions unaddressed."

Robert Scott, author of *The Eldarn Sequence* and *15 Miles*

WHAT WILL HAPPEN IN
eragon
IV

Who Lives, Who Dies,
Who Becomes the Third Dragon Rider and
How Will the Inheritance Cycle Finally End?

Richard Marcus

Ulysses Press

Published in the United States by
Ulysses Press
P.O. Box 3440
Berkeley, CA 94703
www.ulyssespress.com

ISBN: 978-1-56975-728-4
Library of Congress Control Number 2009902107

Acquisitions Editor: Keith Riegert
Managing Editor: Claire Chun
Editor: Kathy Kaiser
Editorial Associates: Lauren Harrison, Kate Kellogg
Production: Abigail Reser
Readers: Alya Javed Hameed, Austin Milot, Ruth Starkman
Design: what!design @ whatweb.com

Printed in the United States by Bang Printing

10 9 8 7 6 5 4 3 2 1

Distributed by Publishers Group West

To my wife Eriana Marcus,
who has been the light of inspiration in my life
for the past thirteen years.

Table of Contents

Acknowledgments

You don't complete a project like this without having had considerable help both before you begin and along the way. There's no way I would have ever even been considered for this project if it hadn't been for the encouragement and advice I've received over the past four years from a variety of people.

First and foremost, I want to thank Ashok Banker for always having time in his own busy schedule for guidance and friendship in equal measure. Robert Scott somehow found time in his insane life to take an interest in my work and at various times over the last four years has offered much needed encouragement and support. I also have to acknowledge the wonderful opportunity that writing for Blogcritics. org has been for improving and refining my writing; I extend my thanks to publisher Eric Olsen, managing editor Lisa

MaKay, and their team of volunteer editors for their support and assistance.

People aren't just formed overnight, and I'm no exception. During the past forty-eight odd (very odd) years there have been various people who have inspired and cajoled me into finding my way. Hersh Jacob taught me what it means to really be an artist and, even more importantly, that the arts are every bit as much a business as any other profession is. Over the course of two very long and far-ranging phone conversations, Willy DeVille taught me what the word "passion" really means and was responsible for my first paid writing gigs. James Barclay, Bob Brozman, Xavier Rudd, Grayson Capps, Chad Umstrum, R. Scott Bakker, Guy Gavriel Kay, Diane Darby, Elizabeth Pasolini, Charlie Ried, Richie Havens, Francis Jockey, Yasmina Khadra, Arlo Guthrie, and others were all generous enough to spend time with me talking about themselves and their art, opening my mind to the different places that inspiration can come from.

Of course, those who have known me the longest are also the ones to whom I owe the most: my brother, David Chalmers, and my mother, Susan Marcus. Without them, I doubt I would even be here today. My wife, Eriana Marcus, has seen both the best and worst of me, and has never stopped believing in me, for which I'll always be eternally grateful.

Then there are those people from Ulysses Press who were responsible for nursing me through the process of actually creating this book. It was acquisitions editor Keith Riegert who took a chance on an unknown author, offered me this opportunity, and shepherded me through the first stages of the book's

Acknowledgments

completion. Managing editor Claire Chun took over halfway through the writing process and showed great patience and good humor in helping quell my panic and explaining what was required to actually finish the project.

Of course, once an author finishes writing, the job is only half done, and it's because of the amazing attention to detail Kathy Kaiser and her editorial staff lavished on my manuscript that it ended up as the polished product you're holding in your hands. Without them, you would have discovered just how many ways there are of spelling Nasuada!

Finally, without the imagination and creativity of one young man there would have been no reason to write this book at all. Plenty of fifteen-year-olds start writing stories, but it takes a special kind of person to not only finish the project but also to have created something as sophisticated and enchanting as the Inheritance cycle. Like many other people, I owe a debt of gratitude to Christopher Paolini for providing me hours of entertainment with his books, and I can only hope that my own modest effort reflects the admiration I have for him and his work.

Bibliography

Christopher Paolini, *Eragon*. Trade Paperback. New York: Alfred A. Knopf, 2005.

Christopher Paolini, *Eldest*. Trade Paperback. New York: Alfred A. Knopf, 2005.

Christopher Paolini, *Brisingr*. Hardcover. New York: Alfred A. Knopf, 2008.

Introduction

It seems only fitting to begin a book of predictions with a prediction, and so I predict that many readers will wonder why anyone would write a book foretelling the plot of someone else's story. Unfortunately, I can, with almost equal certainty, predict that most will answer their own question with another, or perhaps even two: Who the heck is Richard Marcus? And what makes him such an expert on the subject of Eragon? I hope that I can answer these two questions well enough with this introduction that you're encouraged to read the rest of the book to find out why *What Will Happen in Eragon IV* was written.

For close to four years now, I've been a book critic for various online and print publications. This means that I've spent a lot of time reading other people's work and evaluating it by analyzing what type of job they have done in creating a story. I ask myself many questions: Are the characters believable? Has the author done a good job of creating the world that the story takes place in? Why should anybody be interested in reading this story? What has the author done to make it enjoyable to read? In other words, I look for all the details that go into making a story exciting and figure out if the author has done a good job of creating them and putting them all together.

In the case of Christopher Paolini's Inheritance cycle, where there are multiple books involved, I've followed the series from the outset, with an eye for how the author has developed the plot over a sustained period of time. So when, for example, at the end of *Eldest*, Murtagh appears, flying Thorn to battle with Eragon and Saphira (*Eldest* pp. 646–653), I look back to earlier in the story to see if the author simply pulled that out of his hat, or if he laid the groundwork in previous parts of the story.

As any reader of the series will know, Paolini scattered plenty of clues throughout both *Eragon* and *Eldest* to set up the appearance of Murtagh on the back of Thorn, both of them fighting on the side of Galbatorix. In fact, part of the fun of reading the first three books has been trying to figure out what's going to happen based on the clues that the author has dropped into the story. It's the same with any series, from Tolkien's Lord of the Rings to Rowling's Harry Potter books. All those unanswered questions that pop up during the course of a series make the story exciting. The more interesting the questions, the more compelling the series.

I mean, would you have read all seven books of the Harry Potter series if all that were at stake was whether Harry would pass Divination? Or would you have read through to the end of Tolkien's trilogy just to find out whether Sam married Rosie Cotton? Probably not, in either case. Would you be as hooked on the Inheritance cycle if the only thing at stake were whether Eragon was going to be able to help Roran and his uncle get their crop in this year? That wouldn't make for a very compelling novel, let alone a four-book series.

What has impressed me the most as I've been reading and analyzing all three books in the series is how well Paolini has managed to use these various mysteries and questions to pique our interest in the plot, build tension in the story, and keep the conclusion to the series hidden from view. Like any fan of the books, as the series has continued I've had to wonder just how he's going to manage to bring all the elements together in a satisfying conclusion.

Although I know that there were people who were disappointed with Paolini's decision to extend the series to a fourth book, I thought that it showed maturity on his part to realize that rushing the series to a conclusion would be a mistake. *Brisingr* brought readers to the point where they could eagerly anticipate a book that would not only resolve all the burning questions raised in the first three books but perhaps surpass the first three in excitement and adventure. If the author had tried to squeeze everything into *Brisingr*, he could not have built the same type of anticipation or excitement or done justice to the process he began with *Eragon*.

With this book, I hope to offer fellow fans of the series an opportunity to have fun speculating on, and watching me try to figure out the answers to, some of the questions raised

15

throughout the first three books of the Inheritance cycle. There are all sorts of dangling threads to be picked up and woven into the tapestry that Paolini has created. I've gone back through the first three books, hunting for any clues that would enable us to answer the questions that are weighing the heaviest on our minds. Each chapter of this book examines either one of those questions or one of the loose ends, and posits various answers and possible outcomes. In each instance, I'll let you know which answer or outcome I think is the most plausible and try to justify it through my interpretations of the text.

However, that shouldn't stop you from coming to your own conclusions. Feel free to slang me in your blog if you think I'm way off base—but only if you can offer a viable alternative solution and back it up with good, solid evidence. There are two ways that I'll know whether I've done a good job writing this book. One will be if I can convince people that my vision of what will happen is accurate, but equally important, as far as I'm concerned, is if people are encouraged to speculate about what they think will happen as well. I'll be pleased as punch if what I predict in this book is what ends up happening in Book Four, but I'll be almost as happy to be dead wrong and know that I've played some part in motivating people to delve deeper into the series. Half the fun in reading the books has been watching how Paolini has drawn everything together, and I think that it will only increase our fun as readers if we try to anticipate how he will continue that process.

I don't have any special insights into Paolini's process. And I'm not offering him suggestions on how he should finish his book. Think of this book as a love letter from one fan of the series to another, and as a way for all of us to stay involved with the story that has come to mean so much to us over the course of three books and the years it's taken the author to write them. (I'm not mentioning the movie because that's a whole other ball of wax—and not one that I'm interested in peeling open right here and now.)

The object of this book is for us to be able to keep a connection with the world that we've come to enjoy so much, honor the writing of an author whose work we admire, and have a good time doing it. If this book provokes discussion and interest in Paolini's books, all the better. Nothing would make me happier than if you have happened to pick up this book without knowing anything about the Inheritance cycle, and it inspires you to read the books. As all of us who've had the pleasure of reading them can tell you, once you enter the world of the Dragon Riders of Alagaësia, you won't ever want to leave.

Chapter 1

Where We Come In

Although it's probably safe to assume that most readers of this book have at least a passing familiarity with the story line of Christopher Paolini's Inheritance cycle, I still think that it's important to recap the story thus far. One of the most intriguing plot twists involving the series had nothing to do with the story line itself though, but the fact that it was expanded from a trilogy to include a fourth book. It was back in October 2007, when Alfred A. Knopf, an imprint of Random House, the series' publisher, was announcing *Brisingr*'s release date that they also dropped that bombshell.

As most of us who have read the series to date are sure to agree, Paolini's reason for the additional book ("[T]he remainder of the story was far too big to fit in one volume... In order to be true to my characters and to address all of the plot points and unanswered questions *Eragon* and *Eldest* raised, I needed to split the end of the series into two books"), as quoted in the press release, was completely valid. In spite of any initial disappointment you might have felt upon hearing the news, after reading *Brisingr* you really couldn't find any fault in his thinking.

Think back to the end of Book Two, *Eldest*, for a second. Now, how believable would it have been for the character of Eragon, as we saw him then, to be able to grow and learn all that he needed to know to defeat Galbatorix in only one book? Not only would it have gone against everything that the author had worked to establish with the character of Eragon, it would have flown in the face of the lesson that Eragon's teachers had tried to instill in him up to that point: that the development of his character was as important as the development of the power needed to destroy Galbatorix (*Eldest* pp. 273–274).

How many times did Oromis draw back from teaching Eragon something, even though it might provide Eragon with the strength, or the means, for Saphira and him to win their battle, because its utilization would have turned him into a Galbatorix clone? The way that Eragon wins his battle is just as important as the victory itself. Sometimes it's hard for us readers to remember, but Eragon is still only a year or two removed from being the fifteen-year-old farm boy who found a mysterious blue stone in the woods of The Spine (*Eragon* p. 7). Sure, he means well and only wants to see people's suffering end, but he needs to learn the responsibilities that come with power. Look at what happened when he blessed Elva (*Eragon* pp. 428–429). If he made a mistake like that in defeating Galbatorix, he could doom all of Alagaësia!

Where We Come In

I'm jumping around here in my recapping, but it's vital to understand the moral code that Eragon's teachers have instilled in him. Allowing Eragon to take another book to develop as a human being, to learn more about life, is as key an ingredient of the story as any of the plot devices that Paolini brings into play in *Brisingr*. We have to believe that Eragon is capable of defeating Galbatorix, and a big part of that is him attaining a level of emotional and mental maturity that is equal to the physical maturity that he was gifted with during the Agaetí Blödhren under the boughs of the Menoa tree by the Caretakers, Iduna and Nëya, and the magical dragon that their song and dance invoked (*Eldest* p. 469).

As far as Eragon knows, when the story begins in *Eragon*, Book One of the series, he is nothing more than a simple farm boy. Abandoned by his mother and his father unknown, Eragon is living with his uncle and cousin in the small village of Carvahall in the kingdom of Alagaësia. Big changes ensue when, out hunting one day, Eragon discovers a mysterious blue stone that turns out to be the egg that hatches Saphira—the dragon that he is destined to ride. The Dragon Riders had once ruled the land until one of their own betrayed them. Galbatorix gathered a core group of followers to him, the Forsworn, and proceeded to kill other Riders (and their dragons) until he believed there were no surviving Dragon Riders who were capable of challenging him.

Although he has managed to conquer the country, there still exist those who resist him. However, the Varden, the human resistance group, and the elves know that their only hope to defeat Galbatorix lies in a new Dragon Rider coming into existence. Although Galbatorix has killed all the dragons, three eggs remain, awaiting their match—for a dragon egg will hatch only for his or her chosen Rider, even if the dragon egg has to wait a thousand years for that person to come along.

In *Eragon*, our hero begins his quest to become the Dragon Rider who will end the reign of Galbatorix. His initial training is handled by Brom, the man whom Eragon had always known as the village storyteller, but who turns out to be much more. Through Brom, Eragon not only learns the true history of Alagaësia, but he also learns about the Varden, the elves, and the history of resistance against Galbatorix. But Brom is a man of many secrets, one of which is that he was once a Dragon Rider himself and the other—as we find out in Book Three, *Brisingr* (p. 604)—that he is Eragon's father.

It's also in Book One that we first meet Arya, daughter of the queen of the elves. Arya is responsible for Eragon finding the dragon egg that hatches Saphira. After rescuing Arya from the clutches of an evil Shade, Durza, in the employ of Galbatorix (*Eragon* pp. 300–309), Eragon falls hopelessly in love with her. However, it is a love that is seemingly doomed not to be reciprocated and a source of frustration and hurt for Eragon, as there is little hope for a union between an elf and a human.

If Eragon's relationship with Arya is confused, that's nothing compared with the perplexing relationship he has with the person he discovers to be his half-brother, Murtagh. For although the two young men share the same mother, their fathers couldn't have been more different. Murtagh's father, Morzan, was one of the Riders who allied with Galbatorix and was responsible for killing Brom's dragon; Brom, in turn, hunted Morzan down and killed him in vengeance (*Eldest* pp. 280–281). Murtagh had grown up in Galbatorix's court, and the king had hoped that Murtagh would become a Dragon Rider who would serve him, as Murtagh's father had. Although Murtagh managed to escape the king's clutches when he was young and proves to be a loyal ally and faithful companion to Eragon, helping him reach the Varden safely, he is captured again at the beginning of the second book, *Eldest*. Ensnared by Galbatorix through the king's knowledge of his true name, he becomes the king's slave and is revealed at the end of *Eldest* as a Dragon Rider in his service (*Eldest* pp. 646–653).

When Eragon and Murtagh meet in battle at the end of *Eldest*, we discover that Galbatorix doesn't want Eragon killed, as he has sent Murtagh to take him and Saphira alive (*Eldest* pp. 651–652). If he can control all the Dragon Riders, the king will have no problem defeating the Varden and ruling Alagaësia indefinitely. Although Eragon is able to convince Murtagh to let him go at the end of *Eldest*, their fight makes him realize how woefully unprepared he is to battle a mature Dragon Rider in spite of the transformation he has undergone. This realization is reinforced at the beginning of *Brisingr*, when, even aided by twelve elvish spellcasters, he is barely able to fight Murtagh and his dragon, Thorn, to a draw (*Brisingr* pp. 317–329).

However, before he can return to Oromis for further training, Eragon must carry out a mission for the Varden and serve as their representative at the selection of the new king of the dwarves (*Brisingr* p. 361). The dwarves have been one of the Varden's staunchest allies, but when their king is killed by Murtagh in the battle at the end of *Eragon*, the alliance is jeopardized. There are quite a few dwarf clans who oppose having any dealings with the outer world, and don't believe that they should have anything to do with the battle to over-throw Galbatorix. If the Varden were to lose the support of the dwarves, not only would they lose a valuable source of materials, but their armies would also be reduced by nearly half.

Although it all turns out well in the end — Orik, a friend of the Varden, and Eragon's adopted clan brother, is elected king (*Brisingr* p. 543) — the ending is not without strife, as the clan of dwarves most opposed to dealing with the outside world, the Az Sweldn rak Anhûin, attempts to have Eragon assassinated (*Brisingr* pp. 449–454). Their plot is thwarted and the head of the clan is cast out, but the clan is still a potential threat that can't be ignored.

Once Eragon is finished with his mission, he is able to squeeze in a short visit to Oromis for more training. The Varden are about to go on the offensive and desperately need their Dragon Rider, but they also realize that he has to be able to defeat Murtagh and Thorn, not to mention Galbatorix, if they are to have any hope of winning the war in the long run. It's during this training that Eragon learns not only about Brom being his father, but of the existence of a dragon's heart of hearts, Eldunarí, in which a dragon's spirit and power can live on after the dragon dies. Just before Eragon and Saphira leave to rejoin the Varden, Glaedr, who is Oromis's dragon, bequeaths them his heart of hearts.

Where We Come In

It's during *Eldest* that Eragon's cousin Roran takes on a larger role in the story, as Galbatorix sends troops and the Ra'zac after him in an attempt to get at Eragon. Although Roran is able to rally the villagers to fight against the soldiers, his fiancée's father, Sloan, betrays them, with the result that Katrina is taken prisoner by the Ra'zac. Vowing to free her and to make Eragon help him, for he holds him responsible for the mess they are in, Roran convinces the people of Carvahall to follow him across the country to find the Varden and join the fight against Galbatorix. The villagers show up in the nick of time at the end of *Eldest* to help the Varden defeat Galbatorix's army. Then, at the beginning of *Brisingr*, Roran and Eragon are able to rescue Katrina and finally exact vengeance on the Ra'zac by killing both them and their parents.

By the end of *Brisingr*, Roran has risen to become a captain in the Varden. Proving that his ability to lead is not limited to those of his own village or even his own race, he's able to win the respect of the Varden's uneasy ally the Urgals, a fierce race that waged war against humans in the past, but is now an ally with them in the war against Galbatorix. *Brisingr* ends on a sad note, though, as after years of remaining in hiding, Oromis and Glaedr join the elves when they march to war, and although they are able to hold their own against Murtagh and Thorn when they show up on the battlefield, Galbatorix intervenes and gives Murtagh the opportunity to kill them both (*Brisingr* pp. 734–735).

So we end *Brisingr* with the realization that although the Varden are able to have some success on the battlefield, unless Eragon can figure out a way to defeat Galbatorix in a direct confrontation, they are doomed to defeat in the end. However, the death of Oromis has deprived the Varden of not only an esteemed ally but also a valuable source of information on how to defeat Galbatorix. Still, there is reason to hope, as Eragon retains possession of Glaedr's Eldunarí and has access to Glaedr's memories and knowledge to help him in the struggle ahead. Furthermore, he has been given a few ideas and clues as to how he might be able to overcome Galbatorix in a direct battle.

Although Eragon's confrontation with Galbatorix and the defeat of the Empire are the focal points of the series, there are also other matters in the story needing to be resolved as well. It's these threads, which Paolini has woven so masterfully, that make the series more than just the story of a fight between two people. Besides Eragon, there are other characters whom we have grown to care for, and their fates are all still up in the air. There's also the matter of who will rule Alagaësia when the Empire is defeated, who the final dragon egg will hatch for, and a myriad of other issues that need to be resolved. Although some of them might appear trivial when compared with the fate of a country, it's those details that make both the story and its characters so compelling. Anyone who has any concerns about Book Four being anticlimactic has only to think about all that is left to be resolved to know that there is no cause for alarm. Still unconvinced? Perhaps the remaining chapters of this book will persuade you otherwise.

Book Four: When and What Name?

At the time of this writing, *Brisingr*, Book Three of the Inheritance cycle, has been released for only four months. Neither the author nor the publisher has said much about the fourth book, just that it is to be written and that Christopher Paolini has promised to write it as quickly as he can. Of course, the Web is rife with speculation about what will happen in the concluding chapter, but the only official announcements from the author or his publisher have come in the form of the press release announcing the fact that there would be a fourth book and the author's brief mention of the fourth book in the acknowledgments in *Brisingr*.

Although this book is obviously dedicated to trying to predict the plot of Book Four, what about the book itself? When will it be released? And what will it be called? I'm not a mind reader, so I have no way of knowing what's going on in the author's head as he's trying to pull together all the various strands he's left dangling or what kind of writing schedule he's set for himself. As for the title of the fourth and final book of the series, it eludes me also.

Even if I were privy to that sort of information—in fact, even if Christopher Paolini himself were to phone me once a week to let me know how he was progressing and when he expected to be finished—that still wouldn't give us the definitive answer as to when the powers that be at Alfred A. Knopf would release the book into our eager hands. Having been reviewing books for a few years now, I've learned a little of how the industry works. The publishing year runs from September to September, and books are usually released at one of three times during the year: the fall (September to December), winter/spring (January to April), and summer (May to August).

Looking back at the publication history of the Inheritance cycle for clues as to when the fourth book might be published is a little problematic. As many know, Paolini self-published *Eragon* in 2002, prior to it being published by Knopf in August 2003—the end of the summer season. *Eldest* was published two years later on August 25, again at the end of the summer publishing season.

August is an odd time to publish a book for young adults, especially *Eldest*, because the series had already started to prove itself popular. August is the month just before the intended readers return to school, and it is too far in advance of Christmas for people to consider buying it as a present.

However, the folks at Knopf seemed to have learned their lesson with *Brisingr*: its publishing date was the end of September in 2008. (Of course, by then they probably could have published it anytime they wanted and not worried about sales, considering how popular the series had become.)

However, the key fact here is that instead of two years between titles, as with the first books, there was a three-year gap between *Eldest* and *Brisingr*. Now, before anyone starts to panic, thinking that we're going to have to wait until 2011 for the last book to be published, consider the circumstances that went into writing *Brisingr*. Remember that it was only during its writing that Paolini realized that he would have to extend the series to a fourth book, which meant that he probably had to do substantial revisions to the structure of the story.

Revisions might add an extra year onto the process, especially considering that the book would still have to go through the usual editing and proofreading before publication. Having interviewed quite a few authors, I've learned that it can take upwards of a year from the time an author hands in a completed manuscript until it is actually published. Remember that Knopf issued a press release on October 30, 2007, almost a year before *Brisingr*'s publication, announcing that the series would now be four books and that they expected to release *Brisingr* on September 28, 2008. That announcement was followed by a second press release, this one on January 16, 2008, changing the release date to September 20, 2008, and letting us know the title.

What that means is that they most likely had their hands on the completed manuscript—at least a final draft—before the first press release went out in October. This supposition is substantiated by looking back to the October 2007 press release from Alfred A. Knopf announcing that there would be a fourth book. In this press release, the author spoke about Book Three in the past tense.

The good news that we can take away from that same press release is that I seriously doubt that it will take until 2011 for us to see Book Four. In fact, this book might take the author less time than the first three. He must have already planned quite a bit of its plot when he was preparing to write *Brisingr*, and, as any author will tell you, knowing what you want to write is half the battle. For instance, when I sat down to write this chapter, I had already spent some time thinking about it and laying out a plan of attack in my head. So when I sat down to write, all I had to do was write, not wonder what the heck I was going to say.

Therefore, although there's virtually no hope of Book Four appearing in fall 2009, we could see it as early as June 2010. For the reasons I've already stated, it's not feasible to expect the publisher to get Book Four into print only a year after they've released *Brisingr*. There's just too much work that would have to be done, even if Paolini had the manuscript of Book Four completed by the time that *Brisingr* was published. Even June 2010 would be cutting it close, but I think that they could make it if everything goes smoothly.

First of all, they are guaranteed a readership, so they don't have to worry overly much about advance publicity. People were waiting for it to be published even before *Brisingr* was released! Also, June is a great time to release a book for the young adult audience—it will be the beginning of summer vacation for most of the North American and British markets—which means that countless kids will be able to devote their energies to nothing but reading the book. Knopf can announce its release date on the first anniversary of *Brisingr*'s publication, giving them nearly eight months to build up to the release of Book Four.

Now, obviously I could be way off base with this, and they might elect to keep it at two years between release dates, as they did with the first two books. But I think they could score quite a few extra points with readers if they were able to swing the early release date. It would sure take a little of the sting out of having to wait for a fourth book, and make all of us fans happy. So I'm going to go out on a limb and say that June or July 2010 will see the release of Book Four of the Inheritance cycle. I could ask Angela to roll the dragon bones for me, but we all know what a risky business that can be, and I'm not that interested in finding out about my future, thank you very much.

The Title

Now, here's where we get into the serious guesswork. Quite frankly, I was stumped for an idea on this for quite a while. At first glance, the titles of the first three books didn't seem to have anything in common, aside from each of them being only one word. The second stumper was that each of the previous titles was specific to some important aspect of the book: *Eragon* dealt with Eragon, *Eldest* could have referred equally to the elves in general or to Oromis and Glaedr specifically, and, of course, *Brisingr* refers to the new sword forged for Eragon by the elven smith Rhunön, as well as being the word for *fire* in the ancient language.

So you see the conundrum: in order to figure out the title of the fourth book, we need to figure out who or what will play a pivotal role in the story. Because the author can't name the fourth book *Eragon*, and I don't think he would name it after either Murtagh or Galbatorix, no matter how much bearing the character had on the outcome of the series, I think we can pretty much eliminate character names as titles for this book. We might be very fond of both Roran and Arya, but I don't think either one will be deserving of having the book named after him or her.

Once I had eliminated people, and began thinking of objects that could be the title—objects that were only one word long and that were bound to play a key role in the book, the series, and the battle to overthrow Galbatorix—I rapidly came up with a list. This list has only two items: 1) Shur'tugal—the word in the ancient language for Dragon Rider (technically, not a thing); and 2) Eldunarí, "the heart of hearts"—the object in which a dragon can encase its spirit and thus bequeath it to another being.

Of the two, I'm leaning toward the latter because of the degree of significance that Paolini had placed on them in *Brisingr* and because we know that they are one of the major sources of Galbatorix's power. Now that Eragon and Saphira carry Glaedr's Eldunarí with them, and he has passed on, I have to think that this Eldunarí will be of vital importance in helping to win the war. Like the previous titles, this title will have special meaning to the book and to the overall story.

Still, a good case can be made for "Shur'tugal." The first three books have seen Eragon training and preparing to become a Dragon Rider in order to be able to confront and defeat Galbatorix. Not only has Eragon undergone the physical transformation necessary for him to compete on an equal footing with both Galbatorix and Murtagh, he has also grown emotionally and mentally. Paolini has placed a substantial amount of emphasis on this aspect of Eragon's development and has done an excellent job of allowing it to happen gradually. Pretty much everything that Eragon undergoes during the first three books has something to do with his developing into a Dragon Rider.

At the end of *Brisingr*, Eragon is finally confident enough in himself that he feels able to say to Saphira, "We can do this," in reference to defeating Galbatorix and winning the battle for Alagaësia's freedom. He is finally able to call himself Shur'tugal in the truest sense of the word, not just because he happens to ride on the back of a dragon. Because the first book of the series referred to him by name, it would only be fitting if the concluding book referred to Eragon by the title he has finally earned, *Shur'tugal*.

However, I still think that, of the two titles, *Eldunarí* is the most likely, not only for the significance of the object itself, but also for what the saying "heart of hearts" implies. If you know something in your heart of hearts, that means you know it to be the truth. I have a feeling that Eragon is going to have to face up to quite a few of those truths in Book Four, and his ability to do so will be one of the reasons he will be able to defeat Galbatorix. I have a feeling that he will be forced to make a decision that he knows in his heart of hearts is right, but will cause him a great deal of personal pain. However, the decision will also ensure that Galbatorix is overthrown, so he will do what he has to do, no matter what the personal cost.

By listening to his heart of hearts, through the assistance offered by Glaedr's Eldunarí, and perhaps by stealing or somehow else separating Galbatorix from his stash of Eldunarí, Eragon will succeed in his battle to free Alagaësia, and Book Four will carry that word proudly as its title.

Chapter 3

Angela, the Dragon Bones, and Solembum, Too!

One of the characters who is something of an enigma—from the first time we meet her in *Eragon* (p. 179), right on through to the end of *Brisingr*—is the witch Angela. Now, there's no question as to whose side she is on, but she always seems to be holding something back; she seems to know something but, for her own reasons, she's not telling. She also has this uncanny ability to show up in the most unlikely of places in a way that makes you feel that she just might have more power than she's letting on. Mainly, though, she seems to delight in discomfiting people, rattling their confidence in preconceived notions, so that they are made to feel uncomfortable and then are forced to rethink their intentions or ideas.

Nobody—not the elves, the Varden, the dwarves, or Eragon—is quite sure what to make of her, but as all of the former allow her to come and go as she pleases in their inner-most sanctuaries and let her speak her mind, there's not much Eragon can do about her sharp tongue. And if she isn't disconcerting enough on her own, the fact that she has a werecat as a constant companion makes her even more of an oddity. As far as Eragon knows upon first meeting the odd pair, were-cats don't exist, except in stories. And even in those, they are more likely to be talked about than to put in an appearance (*Eragon* p. 200).

The werecat, Solembum, is so similar in character to Angela that it does make you wonder as to the true nature of their relationship. After all, a great many witches have been known to take animal familiars, beings with whom they're linked in arcane ways and with whom they share a deeper bond than is typical for a domesticated animal and a human. In some instances, a witch's or wizard's familiar could be the repository for part of their power. In others, the familiar can communicate with the human over long distances. And in yet others, it's simply the case of two powerful creatures agreeing to join forces and become companions.

It's interesting to note that in some cases the relationship between familiar and human is similar to that of Dragon Rider and dragon; each is acutely aware of what the other is going through at (almost) all times. If, in those circumstances, a familiar were to die, the witch or wizard who was bonded with that familiar would feel like a part of him or her had died. He or she would be seriously weakened for some time. Given how Solembum and Angela are hardly ever seen apart, there is a strong possibility that he is her familiar. (Of course, it also might depend on which of the two you were to ask; Solembum, being an extremely intelligent cat, might insist that Angela is his familiar, not the other way around.)

Part of the mystery of Angela is, of course, the question, What exactly is she? When first we and Eragon meet her in *Eragon*, in the chapter titled "The Witch and the Werecat" (*Eragon* p. 198), she is the owner of a small herb shop in the city of Teirm, "coincidentally" located next door to the house where Brom and Eragon are staying. That the house happens to be the home of Jeod, the merchant who helped recover the egg that Saphira hatched from, is enough to make you wonder how much her location really is a coincidence. Especially when, at the end of their first meeting, she reveals that she not only knows Brom but claims to be aware of the doom that awaits him.

For, as we all know, Angela is a fortuneteller, and the reading she does for Eragon at their first meeting offers the first clues of what lies ahead for Eragon (*Eragon* pp. 203–205). Probably not since the prophecy surrounding a certain teenage wizard has there been a set of predictions discussed and analyzed as much on the Web, and I'm sure most of you have given them some thought already. However, like all fortunes, there is a degree of ambiguity to these predictions that leaves them open to interpretation. And because this is a book trying to get a handle on what will happen to Eragon in Book Four, it seems only fitting that I take a stab at figuring them out. Perhaps some of them have already come true, possibly some of them are ongoing, and maybe some of them might never even come true. The future is uncertain and always subject to change, after all. In the same way that a person can affect their true name by changing their nature, they can alter their future. The future is a malleable thing that can be changed through a person's choices and behavior. So although Angela's predictions for Eragon's future may appear to be referring to something that has already happened in the series, it is equally possible that, through his choices and actions, his future will change. Or the predictions could refer to events that have yet to happen.

When Angela casts the dragon bones, Eragon is surprised when she speaks three words in the ancient language, the language of magic: "Manin! Wyrda! Hugin!" As Eragon has only recently learned, when you use the ancient language in such a way, you call upon the meaning of the word to manifest its power (*Eragon* p. 140). According to the glossary included at the end of *Eragon*, the three words translate as, respectively, "memory," "fate," and "thought." It's interesting to note that the Norse god Odin — who was the father of all the Norse deities, who was also known as Wodin, and from whom we get the word *Wednesday* – was said to own two ravens, who sat upon his shoulders. Their names were Munnin and Hunnin, or "Memory" and "Thought." Each morning they would fly out over the world and then return to Odin to tell him what they saw; he would use that information to try to predict what would happen during the course of the day. Apparently, Paolini has used the ancient Norse language as at least one of the foundations for his ancient language.

As Angela herself says, Eragon's reading is one of the most complicated she has ever come across, and she has to struggle to interpret it (*Eragon* p. 203). For the reading, she casts a set of dragon's knucklebones, each of which is marked with a rune or symbol. Depending on the way the bones are cast, which bones end up next to each other, and which direction they end up pointing, the meaning of each bone can change, or at least be augmented enough, to alter part of its meaning. So although one bone on its own might mean one thing, when combined with another it could take on a totally different meaning.

The first symbol she interprets is a long horizontal line with a circle resting on it—the symbol for infinity or long life—which she says indicates that Eragon will have a long life. In fact, she says she's never seen such a strong indication of long life before, which means he will either be exceptionally long lived or immortal (*Eragon* pp. 203–204). That's pretty straightforward, as by this time Eragon already knows that, as a Rider, he is blessed with an exceptionally long life span, if not immortality. However, after that easy beginning, the messages are increasingly unclear, and although we can see how some of what happens later on in *Eragon*, *Eldest*, and *Brisingr* is foretold here, the predictions are nebulous enough that it's possible for the messages to refer to events that are yet to happen.

The next three bones Angela examines are a good example of this, as even the first bone on its own doesn't predict anything concrete, just a series of hints about what could happen. The wandering-path rune tells her that Eragon will be faced with many choices throughout his life. Battles will be fought over him by the powers in the land, who will seek to control him for their own ends. And although numerous futures are possible for Eragon—all of them filled with blood and conflict—there is one that will bring him great happiness in the end. However, no matter how much people try to control him, Eragon is one of the few people who has control over his own fate. The problem is that it will all come down to the choices he makes, as the flip side of having control over your own destiny is that you can also easily lose your way and make a decision that results in ruin (*Eragon* p. 204). As we have already seen, Eragon doesn't have the greatest track record for making sensible decisions and has been able to escape trouble only through the intervention of others. So this doesn't bode well for him, unless he starts learning to think before he leaps.

Now, one bit of the wandering-path rune becomes clear soon enough, as we see that even among those fighting Galbatorix, there is a struggle to exert control over Eragon and Saphira, especially between the elves and the Varden. Even before Saphira was hatched, control of the egg was an issue; the elves thought that the first new Dragon Rider since the time of the Forsworn should be an elf, as the original Dragon Riders had been. Aside from that, we get the feeling that the elves don't really trust that humans won't become corrupted, as all of the Forsworn had been human. In the end, a compromise was reached, which saw the two groups sharing the egg, and a select group of elves and humans made into couriers responsible for transporting the egg between the two races. As Eragon discovers when he first goes to the elves for training in *Eldest*, a great deal of that resentment still exists among some of the elves. One elf even goes so far as to express his bitterness at the fact that Eragon, and not he, became a Dragon Rider (*Eldest* p. 396).

Angela, the Dragon Bones, and Solembum, Too!

In *Eldest*, and for a while in *Brisingr*, Eragon is forced to maneuver through a minefield of politics that would trouble even the slickest politician. Although in *Eragon*, when he arrives at the Varden's stronghold, he has to ward against the jealousy of magic users, such as the Twins (*Eragon* p. 448), and be careful what he says and to whom, the games start in earnest in *Eldest* when Nasuada succeeds her murdered father as leader of the Varden (*Eldest* p. 15). The ruling council of the Varden try to trap Eragon into binding himself to them in order to turn Nasuada into a figurehead, with the real power residing in their hands (*Eldest* p. 16). Instead, he manages to outwit them by swearing a personal oath of fealty to Nasuada instead of an oath to support the Varden, and the council by implication (*Eldest* pp. 23–24).

Complicated? That's nothing. Compare that with the balancing act he has to perform in order to keep all three peoples (dwarves, elves, and humans) happy, as well as stay true to himself and his goals as a Dragon Rider. Look at the time in *Brisingr* when he has to almost beg Nasuada for permission to spend a little more time among the elves to continue his training (*Brisingr* p. 370). The Varden want to go on the offensive, taking the war to Galbatorix instead of reacting to his attacks, and for that they would need him and Saphira, especially if Murtagh and Thorn were to show up. As he has sworn an oath of fealty to Nasuada and the Varden, Eragon can't refuse Nasuada outright, but if he's to have any chance of fulfilling his destiny as a Dragon Rider, he has to return to the elves.

The whole "What you choose to do will decide your fate" is one of the truly maddening aspects of all fortunetelling. Well, duh, *of course* what you choose to do is going to decide your fate. If you choose to never brush your teeth, not only will you have bad breath but your teeth will fall out in the end, leaving you with an expensive bill for dentures or gumming your food for the rest of your life. We could spend pages upon pages analyzing every choice Eragon has made since the beginning of the series and try to predict how his choices will affect the story's outcome.

Although some of the decisions he has made might still have bearing on the outcome of Book Four—his decision to spare Sloan, Katrina's father, in *Brisingr* (p. 56), for example, or blessing Elva in *Eragon* and then attempting to reverse the blessing in *Brisingr* (pp. 265–266), or even killing the Ra'zac near the beginning of *Brisingr* without finding out what it meant when it said that Galbatorix was getting close to learning "the true name" (*Brisingr* p. 65)—Paolini has given us sufficient examples of the consequences of Eragon's rash decisions that we know that Eragon has to be careful about his choices from here on in to the end of the story.

The next two bones Angela looks at—the sailing ship, indicating a long journey, touching the lightning bolt, signifying bad luck—mean that eventually Eragon is going to have to leave Alagaësia and spend the rest of his life in exile (*Eragon* p. 204). One reason for that would, of course, be if he ended up having to flee for his life in order to escape Galbatorix. But even when the bones were being cast, this looked highly unlikely. To my mind, especially when taken together with the next bone, there's really only one answer to the question of why he would leave Alagaësia forever.

Angela, the Dragon Bones, and Solembum, Too!

The "rose blossom inscribed between the horns of a crescent moon" indicates "[a]n epic romance...extraordinary, as the moon indicates—for that is a magical symbol—and strong enough to outlast empires. I cannot say if this passion will end happily, but your love is of noble birth and heritage. She is powerful, wise, and beautiful beyond compare" (*Eragon* p. 205). Of course, the immediate answer as to who that mysterious person will be is Arya. Not only is she beautiful beyond compare, she's the daughter of the queen of the elves, immortal, powerful, and wise.

If both she and Eragon survive the war that's coming, it would make sense for them to leave Alagaësia to live among the elves, as she will one day have to rule there. It would also work out fine for Eragon, for he would not only marry the woman of his dreams, but he and Saphira would be perfectly positioned to take over the role of teacher of all Dragon Riders. Remember, ever since his physical transformation, when he received the gift of the dragons during the Agaetí Blödhren (*Eldest* p. 469), Ergaon has been more elf than human anyway, so combined with his immortality, he's not exactly going to blend in well with human society.

All that sounds great, but there's a slight hitch. Arya has refused every advance Eragon has ever made toward her. In *Eldest*, following his physical transformation, when he thinks that now that they are the same physically, she might be more amenable to the idea of loving him, she brings up the gap in their life experience, which just can't be overcome:

*"Eragon, this cannot be. You are young and I am
old, and that shall never change....You and I are not
meant for each other."* (*Eldest* pp. 473–474)

When he continues to press her, going so far as to suggest
that she surrender her memories to him as a way of bridging
the gap, she reacts quite predictably:

*"It would be an abomination...Hear me well
Eragon. This cannot be, nor shall never be"...Then
she strode past and vanished into Du Weldenvarden.*
(*Eldest* p. 474)

Now, although in *Brisingr*, she does appear to be softening
somewhat and explains why she has steeled herself against
feelings toward others, nothing has really changed in their
relationship, especially when it comes to the gap in their ages.
Angela never made any promises as to his relationship ending
happily, remember—but what if it wasn't Arya whom the
bones were referring to in the first place? She is merely the
first woman that Eragon develops a crush on as a teenager,
and how many guys end up marrying the girl that they were
besotted with when both were teenagers anyway? After all,
she's not the only beautiful, powerful, and noble woman he
knows, is she? A case could be made that the prophecy is referring to Nasuada, the leader of the Varden.

The main objection to a relationship between Nasuada and
Eragon is, of course, the fact that she isn't an immortal like he
is, but what if the final dragon egg is destined for her? Then
not only would she become immortal, it would also give her a
reason for leaving the Varden, as she would have to travel to

the land of the elves to be trained by Eragon. Although some might see her as the future ruler of Alagaësia, I have the feeling that after having led the Varden and playing the political games that required, she might be happy not becoming queen; in fact, it might even be a relief to leave the royal life behind. There are plenty of other people around who could become king or queen.

I think that if this scenario were to play out, it wouldn't be until near the end of the book, and she would represent the next stage of Eragon's life. The war would be over, he would be preparing to teach any new Dragon Riders that came along, and Nasuada would be his first student. This scenario would be a new beginning in more ways than one.

The final knuckles that Angela reads are the tree and the hawthorn root, "which cross each other strongly. I wish that this were not so — it can only mean more trouble — but betrayal is clear. And it will come from within your own family" (*Eragon* p. 205). Eragon's immediate reaction is to blurt out Roran's name and then insist that betrayal from him is not possible. Of course, at the time, he doesn't know that he has a half-brother, Murtagh, and that Murtagh will become a Dragon Rider serving Galbatorix.

Except there's a problem there, because Murtagh doesn't betray Eragon. Murtagh has no control over what has happened. And, in fact, at the end of *Eldest*, he manages to find a way to stay loyal to his friendship with Eragon and disobey Galbatorix by letting Eragon and Saphira escape after he and Thorn have defeated them in battle. So could there be another betrayal from within the family? Although it's doubtful that

Roran would do anything against Eragon on purpose, what if Katrina were to be captured by Galbatorix again? What wouldn't Roran do to get her back or to keep her from harm? What if they both are captured, and Galbatorix threatens to torture Katrina?

Then there's the fact that Katrina doesn't know that her father is still alive or what Eragon has done to him. How do you think she'd feel if she found out? Maybe she wouldn't feel strongly enough to seek out the means to betray Eragon, but she also might not be so difficult to persuade to spill the beans either. After all, Eragon has lied to her about her father and is responsible for his torment. Even the elves thought it would have been a better idea for Eragon to kill him than to impose that sentence on him.

Now, Angela wasn't the only one passing on cryptic messages during Eragon's visit to the herb shop. Just as he's about to leave, Solembum gives him the following message: "When the time comes and you need a weapon, look under the roots of the Menoa tree. Then, when all seems lost and your power is insufficient, go to the Rock of Kuthian and speak your name to open the Vault of Souls" (*Eragon* p. 206). Despite the fact that the answer to the first part of that riddle was revealed in *Brisingr* with the forging of Brisingr, the sword made from the lump of star metal taken from beneath the Menoa tree in the kingdom of the elves (*Brisingr* pp. 661–677), the second part still remains a mystery.

Could the Vault of Souls be another repository of hearts of hearts? What else could Eragon derive enough power from to defeat Galbatorix? Now, as to the issue of the name, the question is, Which name would he have to speak? I have a feeling that he's going to need to discover his own true name, the name that describes him, in order to open this particular portal. One hitch is finding this place. Another hitch is pulling himself out of a battle to do so. If there is now the risk of both Murtagh and Galbatorix showing up on the battlefield, how can Eragon leave the Varden to face them? They might have gotten away with disguising his absence once (*Brisingr* p. 362), but that was still in the early stages of the war, before the Varden went on the offensive and began attacking cities whose leaders followed Galbatorix. They aren't going to be able to spare Eragon during a battle—what defense would they have against dragons, aside from him?

As Angela said, predicting the future is a very imprecise art, especially with something as nebulous as the bones, but this chapter does provide us with a good set of clues as to what we should be thinking about when considering Eragon's future. It gives us a couple of hints that, when combined with knowledge culled from the pages of the series, suggest a few other possible directions that Paolini could take the story in Book Four. All in all, though, Angela's forecasts are fun to speculate on, but they don't provide any real answers as to Eragon's future. What we can take away from her words is that, in the end, Eragon's future will be what he makes it—and he carries the fate of all free people in his hands. No pressure, though.

Chapter 4

Roran

When we first meet Roran in Book One of the Inheritance cycle (*Eragon* p. 20), he appears to be no more than an incidental character. He's been Eragon's surrogate older brother, and, seemingly, his one friend in what has otherwise been a lonely life. When Roran departs to work in a neighboring town's mill, it appears, what with the way events unfold, that Eragon will never see him again. Combined with the death of Garrow, his uncle (*Eragon* p. 90), it only serves to reinforce Eragon's isolation, leaving him no one to turn to for comfort but Saphira, and making it easy for him to leave home with Brom to seek vengeance on the Ra'zac. As far as the reader can tell, Roran is still alive, but it doesn't appear that he'll have anything more to do with Eragon's story.

So it is somewhat surprising to have Roran not only show up again in Book Two but also become as important a part of the tale as his younger cousin (*Eldest* p. 29). Although the narrative of Roran leading the villagers of Carvahall in resistance against the Ra'zac and the troops sent to capture him, and then herding them across the breadth of the country in order to join the Varden and attempt to rescue Katrina, is exciting and well written, it really is extraneous to the central plot of the series. Christopher Paolini could very well have told the story of Eragon becoming a Dragon Rider without Roran in the script after the first time we meet him. So there has to be an important reason for him to have gone out of his way to make Roran such a prominent character.

Of course, Roran does represent a means for Galbatorix to gain control over Eragon, for if he had succeeded in capturing him, the king could have used threats against Roran's life to force Eragon to capitulate. Or at least Galbatorix could have used Roran as bait to lure Eragon into a trap while attempting to rescue his cousin. The one element introduced into the story that couldn't have been managed without the inclusion of Roran's story is the narrative of Katrina's father, Sloan, and the potential for danger there. Certainly, Roran killed the Twins during the battle of the Burning Plains (*Eldest* p. 648), brought Jeod to the Varden, and provided the motivation and means for Eragon to kill the Ra'zac and their parents, but it would have been easy enough for Paolini to have found ways that those events could have taken place without Roran. This means that either Roran or Sloan has some key role to play in the action still to come.

When Eragon helped Roran rescue Katrina from the Ra'zac, he was left with the problem of what to do with Sloan (*Brisingr* p. 56). Eragon sent him off to live with the elves in the hope that the man would be able to find a way to heal himself of the bitterness and hatred that he felt toward the world for taking his wife from him (*Brisingr* pp. 90–92). Although his love for his daughter is real, it's not very healthy, as he became obsessed with her when his wife died, to the point of being overprotective and jealous of anyone else showing her affection. By the time he betrayed the villagers of Carvahall to the Ra'zac, he had become nearly insane from anger and fear of losing her, which was why he was so willing to sell his neighbors out. He might have been a snob and unfriendly before, but the news that Katrina was betrothed to Roran seemed to completely unhinge him (*Eldest* p. 185).

Even after Eragon frees Sloan from the Ra'zac's clutches, and although Sloan has lost his sight, Sloan's attitude remains unchanged. He may not be as crazed with anger and fear as he was before, but he remains disdainful of Eragon, referring to him as Son of None, a reference to the fact that the villagers always considered him an orphan at best, and an illegitimate child at worst (*Brisingr* p. 78). When Eragon sends him off to stay among the elves, he does so in the hope that living with them, surrounded by peace and beauty, Sloan will be able to heal from all that troubles him and find some peace. However, when he makes his quick visit to Ellesméra in *Brisingr* for some final training, he finds that Sloan has not changed at all. He's still a bitter and angry man who prefers to wallow in his own misery, even though in his rare moments of calm he admits that he feels as if he's choking on his memories (*Brisingr* p. 688).

Unfortunately, this means that he is also still capable of causing damage to both Eragon and Roran if given the means. True, Eragon's spells prevent him from ever leaving Ellesméra, but that doesn't mean there's no chance of him being able to conduct some sort of mischief. What if Galbatorix were to learn of him and somehow find a way to let Roran and Katrina know that he yet lived? What kind of dissent would that sow between the cousins? This is the same man who was so (metaphorically) blinded by his hatred for Roran that he couldn't see the danger he was placing his daughter in when he allowed the Ra'zac to take her. If somehow Galbatorix were to contact him, don't you think that Sloan would delight in causing harm to Eragon and Roran? Especially if he thought it would allow him to get his beloved Katrina back? Sloan might appear to be out of harm's way, and harmless, but remember that Galbatorix's reach is long and the limits to his power unknown. And Sloan is a bitter and vengeful man; we may not have seen the last of him.

Now, of course, there must have been more of a reason for creating the whole Roran/villagers story line than just to introduce Sloan and his potential for troublemaking into the plot. This means that Paolini must have plans for Roran, aside from him being a fierce warrior and captain in the employ of the Varden. In a future chapter, we'll look at the possibility of the final dragon egg hatching for him. But, primarily because of his love for Katrina, that's highly unlikely, so there must be something else in store for him—and not necessarily something pleasant either. I don't think Galbatorix will attempt to get at him again through Katrina. Roran and Eragon have proven that they are more than capable of breaking into even his most carefully guarded sanctuaries to rescue her, and the price for capturing her the first time was the loss of four of his most valuable servants. So Katrina is most likely as safe as anyone can be during a time of war, especially because Eragon has placed wards around her, protecting her from being harmed by normal weapons. But there's nothing saying that Roran won't be in danger.

Although he is a fearsome warrior, Roran also has a tendency to get caught up in the heat of the battle. Look at how he took on close to a hundred of the Empire's soldiers single-handedly in one of his most recent scouting missions (*Brisingr* pp. 522–524). That's not exactly the behavior of someone calm and rational when it comes to battle. And despite the fact that his opponents could come at him only one at a time, fighting so many individual battles in a row could easily have tired him sufficiently for somebody to overcome him, or he could have slipped and fallen and found himself at their mercy. Yet instead of having one of the other men with him relieve him occasionally, he fought until he was completely unaware of anything except the next person in front of him who needed to be killed.

In that situation, he escaped with only minor injuries. But if he continues to fight with that sort of intensity, he might find himself alone on the battlefield with no one guarding his back. Even the bravest warrior can be brought down by a knife, or an arrow in the back. If the wards Eragon puts around him during battle should happen to slip for some reason—Eragon moving out of range, or having to draw upon all of his power in the midst of a battle—he would be just as susceptible to injury as anybody else. However, I seriously doubt that Roran has come this far only to fall under regular battlefield circumstances. If he were to die in battle, it would have ramifications far beyond his own death.

Somehow, I think that the fates of Roran, Murtagh, and Eragon are intertwined, and that Roran will play a key role in deciding how it all turns out. I can't see Eragon being able to kill Murtagh without something happening that pushes him into an unthinking rage. Although it would be nice to think that, somehow or other, Roran would be able to kill Murtagh in battle, the chances of that happening are slim. This means it's far more likely that Murtagh will kill Roran and, in doing so, push Eragon over the edge, making him so angry that he, in turn, kills Murtagh. It wouldn't be surprising if, in fact, Murtagh were to do that deliberately, as a means of getting Eragon angry enough to kill him. For although Murtagh is unable, or unwilling, to change enough to escape Galbatorix, he might be desperate enough to escape him by creating the means to bring about his own death. What surer way to guarantee that Eragon will kill him is there than killing Roran—well, maybe if he were to kill Arya or Nasuada, that would do it, too—but neither of them are as potentially expendable as Roran.

There is another possible, more cheery, scenario for Roran, one that doesn't involve his death, although it does rely on a few other things falling into place. However, it would fit into the picture that Paolini has started to draw of Roran as a charismatic leader, capable of leading his men both by example and through his ability to plan. Somebody is going to have to take over the rule of Alagaësia following the overthrow of Galbatorix. That somebody will not only have to be able to inspire people to work together to rebuild the country, but be strong enough to ensure that recriminations are kept to a minimum after a war that saw horrible acts of violence carried out by both sides.

A civil war, with neighbor pitted against neighbor, is a very divisive war and difficult for a country to recover from. In this case, there will also have been quite a number of people who did well under the rule of the king, who will be resented and hated by those who suffered during that reign and who would want to exact vengeance against them. The only way to prevent a bloodbath under these circumstances is to have a leader who is strong enough to convince people that there is a better way of doing things than slitting the throats of the people they have disagreed with. Of course, there will still have to be a means of meting out justice against those who really did cause suffering, but in order for the country not to be torn apart, it can't be carried out by lynch mobs.

On top of this, the new leader will also have to work out how to best integrate the various races of people who now inhabit the land. Most humans have little or no experience with dwarves and elves, and are as liable to be afraid of them as they are willing to live with them. Even more important is the fact that whoever the new leader is, he or she is going to have to deal with the integration of the Urgals as well — especially after the role they have played in helping overthrow Galbatorix. If people have suspicions about dwarves and elves, that's nothing compared with how they are going to feel about the Urgals. One only needs to look at Eragon's bigoted attitude toward them before he scanned Garzhvog, leader of those who allied with the Varden (*Eldest* pp. 618–619), to begin to understand how the human population in general are going to feel about them.

Of course, part of the problem lies with the Urgals and the way their society is currently structured. It is based on respect for the most powerful, the one who can prove himself in battle over others. Garzhvog, who is head of the Krull, the warrior society of the Urgals, and who makes up part of Nasuada's bodyguard, has admitted to Eragon that he knows this is something that's holding the Urgals back. If they can't figure out another way of establishing status and proving themselves worthy of mates, they won't survive as a species (*Brisingr* p. 392). However, in order for the Urgals to be integrated, and perhaps learn how to change their ways, there will need to be a leader in Alagaësia who has their respect because of his or her strength, but who will also set them an example of how it is possible to be tough without fighting all the time.

So far, only three characters have been able to earn the respect of the Urgals in that way: Eragon, Nasuada, and Roran. As the Urgals are used to being led by women — they are ruled by a group of females called the Herndall (*Eldest* p. 609) — Nasuada is, naturally enough, accepted by them as a leader, but she has also earned their respect through her strength of mind and her willingness to negotiate with them. However, it is unlikely that she would be able to gain the same position of authority over the entire race of Urgals, simply *because* she is a female, and the Herndall who lead the tribes might have a problem with that.

Naturally, as a warrior race, the Urgals place a great deal of emphasis on martial prowess, especially unarmed combat without the aid of magic. The only human so far in the story who has stood up to a challenge issued by an Urgal has been Roran, when he was sent out with a mixed war party of humans and Urgals. By accepting the conditions of an Urgal's challenge and then defeating that Urgal, Roran was able to win over the entire war party and get them to accept his leadership (*Brisingr* pp. 589–595).

By the end of *Brisingr*, Nasuada has made Roran one of her captains and given him responsibility for leading a part of her army. As the war continues, if he continues to show the type of leadership and bravery that he has already demonstrated, his stature among the Varden will continue to increase and he will take on more and more responsibilities when it comes to fighting the war. Although Nasuada has proven herself to be a remarkable leader—knowing when to take risks and when to play it safe, and figuring out ways of keeping her people fed and occupied when they are not actually fighting battles—the chances of her wanting to take over the governing of Alagaësia after the war are slim. She will most likely want to move on to something else after all that she's been through. Consider the fact that for most of her life she's either been training for leadership or being a leader; she must be getting tired of the responsibilities and want a life of her own.

So who does that leave as potential leaders of Alagaësia, aside from Roran? Although I'm sure that there are many among the Council of Elders in the Varden who think they would be right for the job, and some who believe that Orrin, the king of Surda, the country that has sheltered and supported the Varden, would make a good candidate, none of them would command the same respect as Roran. He has earned the respect needed to lead the country through the tribulations it's sure to undergo while recovering from the civil war.

Of course, it doesn't hurt that he's also related to the Dragon Rider who led Alagaësia to victory over Galbatorix. Aside from the reflected glory, there is also the fact that with Roran on the throne it ensures a connection between Alagaësia's rulers and the next generation of Dragon Riders. For if Roran and Katrina become the new leaders of Alagaësia, their family line will become the new royal family, which means that there will always be a blood tie between the throne and the Dragon Riders.

That connection becomes even more important when you consider that Eragon will be taking up the mantle of teacher to the next generation of Dragon Riders in Ellesméra, and possibly even raising a family of his own, who might be counted among future Riders. Not only does Eragon represent a connection among the human kings in Alagaësia, the Dragon Riders, and the elves, he's also considered a member of the same clan as the current dwarf king, Orik. For the first time in a long time, all of the races living in Alagaësia will at least be talking to one another and have a say in how the country is to be run.

There has to be a reason why Paolini decided to give Roran as large a role as he's ended up having in the books.

Even before he became the leader he has developed into, he was already important to Eragon because he was his only remaining family member. Not only that, but we know that Eragon thinks the world of his cousin, judging by how devastated he was when Roran announced he was leaving home in *Eragon* (p. 56). However, that's not sufficient reason for giving him the substantial role he ends up with, so it can be safely assumed that there is something important awaiting Roran in Book Four.

Unfortunately, he can be equally important to the series dead or alive, so it can't be guaranteed that he'll make it through to the end. Hopefully, for those of you who've become fans of Roran, and, of course, for Eragon's and Katrina's sake, Roran will come out the other side of this war alive, and end up being the ruler of people that he looks to be capable of becoming. It would be awful to see all of his struggling wasted, with him dying under Murtagh's sword, and coming this far in the books, only to serve as an excuse for Eragon to kill his half-brother in revenge for killing the cousin who was like a brother to him. Family can be complicated enough as it is; nobody needs that kind of exasperation, least of all Eragon.

Chapter 5

Murtagh

Fate can play the cruelest of tricks on people. For proof, you don't have to look any further than what happens to the character of Murtagh in Christopher Paolini's Inheritance cycle. As the son of Morzan, the first and most deadly of Galbatorix's thirteen allies, the Forsworn, he was kept a virtual captive. First he was held by his father in order to prevent the other Forsworn from using Murtagh against him. After Morzan's death, he was held by the king. The king kept him close and had him trained as a warrior in the hope that one day, one of his three precious dragon eggs would hatch for the son of his longtime ally. His plan was for Murtagh to become the first of what he hoped to be a new generation of Dragon Riders, who would be completely under his control and whom he could use to finally crush any resistance to his rule (*Eragon* pp. 387–391).

However, Murtagh was braver and angrier than Galbatorix had figured, and he was able to escape the king's clutches before those plans came to fruition. Knowing full well that he would be unwelcome among the Varden because of his heritage, Murtagh was forced into exile, and sought shelter at the estate of an old friend. While he was in hiding, he paid attention to every rumor he heard in the hope of uncovering the king's plans and how they affected him, and he tried to figure out just what he was going to do with his life. It's one thing, after all, to have escaped from the king, and quite another to stay out of his clutches for an extended period. It was during this time that he heard that the Ra'zac had been sent out to either capture or kill somebody. Knowing that Galbatorix would send the Ra'zac after any potential Rider or a dragon, he began trailing them on the off chance that they would find somebody.

At least, that was the explanation he offered to Eragon and Saphira (*Eragon* p. 391), and it was for that reason that he was on the scene and able to rescue Eragon when the Ra'zac had captured Eragon and Brom (*Eragon* p. 264). Although he wasn't in time to prevent the evil creatures from inflicting a mortal wound on Brom, he was able to help Saphira and Eragon move to safety, and assist them in their travels while Eragon recovered from the wounds he received from the Ra'zac. He kept the secret of his heritage hidden from Eragon for as long as he possibly could, but he was finally forced to reveal that there was more to him than met the eye.

Eragon first started to wonder about him shortly after they met, when Murtagh recognized Zar'roc and named it as the sword once belonging to Morzan, something that Eragon hadn't known (*Eragon* p. 280). The fact that Murtagh wasn't any more eager to join up with the Varden than he was to run into representatives from the Empire was equally odd, as was his ability to shield his mind from magical probes. If Eragon hadn't been so preoccupied with dealing with the death of Brom, his injuries, and his quest to find the Varden, he might have been more suspicious. But as it was, he was grateful for Murtagh's help and his companionship.

He became even more grateful to his new friend when, after Eragon was captured by Durza, Murtagh not only helped Saphira free him, but helped to free Arya as well (*Eragon* p. 309). Although Murtagh resisted, he finally agreed to accompany Eragon, Saphira, and a comatose Arya on their trip to the Varden, but only on the condition that he would leave them before they joined up with those leading the resistance. Unfortunately, the choice was taken away from him when they were overtaken by a war party of Urgals, and he was forced to seek whatever shelter he could among the Varden. Needless to say, he had been correct in his worry about the Varden not trusting him. Murtagh was imprisoned as soon as they discovered his identity, primarily for his own protection (*Eragon* p. 405).

However, he wasn't imprisoned for long, as the Varden soon found themselves under attack by Urgals, led by the Shade Durza. Murtagh was freed to help the Varden fight off the invasion. His valor in that fight convinced the Varden to trust him, and it seemed that Murtagh might have found a place where he could be accepted. Unfortunately, the Varden were betrayed by two of their most powerful spellcasters, the duo known only as the Twins, who led a party of Urgals into their fortress. In the ensuing battle, Nasuada's father, Ajihad, leader of the Varden, was killed, and so apparently was Murtagh (*Eldest* p. 6). Of course, as we learn at the end of *Eldest*, it might have been better if he had been killed. For the invaders were under specific instructions to capture Murtagh alive, so that he could be taken back to the Empire and Galbatorix could carry out his original intention for him: enslaving him and forcing him to become a Dragon Rider in the service of the Empire (*Eldest* p. 647).

Murtagh and Eragon both grew up without their parents. As we found out, they had the same mother (*Eldest* p. 652), but they lived very different lives as children, which went a long way toward shaping the people they became. As an orphan, Eragon was, in some ways, as much an outsider as Murtagh, but he at least was raised in an environment where love and respect were present. Murtagh's only memory of his father is carried on his back in the shape of a scar that was caused when his father threw the sword Zar'roc at him. Hated and mistreated by his father, and then raised at court by the king to be his tool, all that kept Murtagh going was his anger at the way he was treated. While he was on the run, the focus of his anger was Galbatorix and the memory of his father, but once he and Thorn were enslaved by Galbatorix, his anger and resentment became directed at fate and at a world that would allow this to happen to him:

"Let go of my anger?" Murtagh laughed. "I'll let go of my anger when you forget yours....Anger defines us, Eragon, and without it, you and I would be a feast for maggots" (*Brisingr* p. 320).

Those words were part of his response to Eragon's suggestion that Murtagh would be able to free himself from Galbatorix's control if he were only to change his nature, and thus change the meaning of his true name (*Brisingr* p. 318). Although he could see the merit of the idea, Murtagh's initial reaction was defensive. He protested that he had done the best he could and thought of himself as a good man. In fact, he was so convinced that he had done his best, he thought the only way he could change his nature significantly enough to change his name would be for him to become as evil as Galbatorix.

Murtagh is too caught up in his own battle against the world and fate to see that it is because he is so one-dimensional, a being filled with anger and nothing else, that it made it so easy for the king to figure out his nature and his true name. It also didn't help matters that the king has kept a close eye on him since he was born and probably knows more about him than I'll bet Murtagh knows about himself. Although Murtagh says that Galbatorix had little to do with him until he was eighteen and summoned him into his presence, I'm sure the king was pulling many of, if not all, the strings behind the scenes, dictating Murtagh's life as a child.

Galbatorix could easily have fostered the environment that allowed a younger Murtagh to grow up lonely and scared, which would develop over the years into anger and resentment at being left alone. There's a great deal of self-pity in Murtagh, expressed in the bitterness and resentment he feels toward Eragon because their mother was able to rescue Eragon from palace life, while Murtagh was stuck there (*Brisingr* p. 319). Of course, at the time when Murtagh was asking Eragon how he thought he would have made out if he'd been raised in the palace, they still thought that they were both Morzan's sons. Obviously, there was no way that their mother would have let Brom's son grow up in the palace, especially when she was able to take him to be raised by her brother in the village where Brom was living. However, Murtagh couldn't know this, and so he thought only of the fact that Eragon had an easier time of it than he had, and perhaps that their mother favored him. Yet from the sound of it, once Morzan was dead, Murtagh's life wasn't really all that bad. Remember, unlike Eragon, who was living the life of a poor subsistence farmer whose family barely had enough money to buy meat, Murtagh was being brought up in the lap of luxury as a favored member of Galbatorix's court.

On top of that, he was being groomed as a potential Dragon Rider, which meant that he was receiving the type of education that most people in Alagaësia could only dream of receiving. Remember how surprised Eragon was, when he and Murtagh first met, that Murtagh was able to shield his thoughts from him? It was merely one of the many things that he would have been taught while living at court, along with reading and writing, and how to fight properly. Eragon, on the other hand, doesn't even start to read until he is fifteen, when Brom is forced to teach him out of necessity during their travels (*Eragon* pp. 210–211). It also doesn't sound as if Murtagh was as alone or friendless as he wants us to believe.

If you remember, before he set out on the road, Murtagh was sheltered by someone who was a good-enough friend to risk Galbatorix's displeasure by hiding him. I doubt that the king would have been forgiving of anybody who interfered with his plans, which means that whoever that person was, he or she had put himself or herself at risk by keeping Murtagh safe from Galbatorix.

It also sounds as though other people were loyal to Murtagh, including the servant who not only trained him as a fighter, but ended up being willing to die for him when Murtagh escaped from the palace. So despite the fact that his life was by no means ideal, it still wasn't as awful as it could have been. In fact, it wasn't until Galbatorix revealed himself to be a heartless dictator, and demanded that Murtagh lead a troop of soldiers out to destroy an entire village, that Murtagh even thought that there was anything wrong with Galbatorix being king. Sure, that had a lot to do with the king's ability to deceive people. But Murtagh must have enjoyed his time at court somewhat if he was willing to listen to and accept the king's vision of a new era of Dragon Riders ruling the country and his notion that the Varden were the ones responsible for all the troubles in the land. Remember that even after he left the king, he wanted nothing to do with the Varden, not only because of who he was but because he thought they were out to destroy the country (*Eragon* p. 391).

Murtagh is one of those people who bemoan their fate, but at the same time are unwilling to try to do anything about it. They would much rather sit back and be angry at the world, and find someone else to blame for their problems, rather than make the effort required to overcome them. They may not enjoy their lives, but it's what they are used to, and they don't see the point in making any changes. Although he is being controlled by Galbatorix, he also doesn't seem to be fighting too hard against him. During their first battle, he even says to Eragon that all the king wants to do is reinstitute the rule of the Dragon Riders—as though the Dragon Riders were a thing of the past. He doesn't seem to think that's necessarily a bad thing, in spite of the fact that Galbatorix would ultimately be in charge. In fact, for a person who is supposedly doing things against his will, he seems downright enthusiastic about his job. Nothing compelled him to deliberately target the king of the dwarves, but during the first battle he picked him out from among all the other fighters on the field to kill (*Eldest* p. 639). True, he doesn't take Eragon and Saphira prisoner during their first battle, but that's only because Eragon, citing their former friendship, convinces him not to. Even so, the only reason he doesn't take them prisoner is that he was only ordered to "try" to capture the two of them, and he could say that he did try. He promises Eragon that the next time they meet, he won't be anywhere near as merciful, as he's sure that Galbatorix will force him to swear even more vows in the ancient language, binding him to that task specifically (*Eldest* pp. 651–652).

If you're looking for clues as to how much his bitterness and self-loathing have taken over his thought processes, look no further than what he says just after he's agreed to not capture Eragon and Saphira in *Eldest*: "If I have become my father, then I will have my father's blade," he proclaims as he steals Zar'roc away from Eragon at the end of that first battle (p. 652). Of course, there are also clues that he might not be such an unwilling servant of the king as well, such as when he boasts of all the magic that Galbatorix has taught him, the ways of using power that can give him anything he wants and destroy his enemies within an instant. These are the spells and the types of magic that Oromis has refused to teach Eragon because they are so evil that they shouldn't be used. But Murtagh takes great pride in the fact that he knows them, and derides the elves and Brom as weaklings for refusing to use them (*Eldest* p. 648).

The last we see of Murtagh is his battle at the end of *Brisingr* with Glaedr and Oromis, in which, just before Galbatorix takes control of him, he rails against the elf for not making himself available to help him (*Brisingr* p. 731). As usual, he's blaming someone else for his misfortune, for there's no way that Oromis could have helped him without running the risk of revealing to Galbatorix that he and Glaedr were still alive. Anyway, Murtagh has a funny way of showing that he wants help. At the same time that Murtagh is upbraiding Oromis for not helping him, he's trying to kill Oromis (*Brisingr* p. 731).

Although it's true that both he and Thorn are confused and scared, Murtagh has yet to show himself willing to do anything to help himself. It's as though he expects the world to help him. He's too enmeshed in his own anger and resentment to see anything beyond his own troubles or be willing to do anything about them. There are some people who become so comfortable with the way they are, no matter how much it's harming them, that they see change as something dangerous. Murtagh has reached that point of no return, it seems, and it really looks as though he will be unable to carry out the changes in himself that are required if he ever wants to be free of Galbatorix.

Perhaps he will find a way to redeem himself before the end, but if he does, it won't come about because of any willingness on his part to admit that there's anything wrong with him. However, I fear that he is now too far gone for even that to occur and that he is destined to cause both Eragon and Saphira still further grief. He's already killed Hrothgar and killed Oromis, so it appears to be only a matter of time before someone else dear to Eragon dies at Murtagh's hands. Unfortunately, Murtagh has fulfilled the destiny that Galbatorix had in mind for him from his birth—becoming his father's son. Although fate can be pitiless and play nasty tricks on humans, we do have some control over our destinies, that is, if we are willing to exercise our free will in order to cause change to happen. By resigning himself to being his father's son, Murtagh has allowed that fate to come true. As Eragon has become the first of a new generation of Dragon Riders dedicated to the original high principles of the calling, Murtagh has become the first of a new generation of the Forsworn.

Chapter 6

Arya: The Proud Princess

Elves have fascinated humans and held a special place in our imaginations since the days before stories were even written down. The fair folk, the neighbor under the hill, the little people, the fairies, the fey, and countless other names have been given to these mysterious beings, whose resemblance to humans ends with the fact that we both walk erect on two legs and have two arms, two eyes, and two ears. Everything else, from the shape of their eyes and their ears to their life spans, are as different from us as if they were covered in fur and walked on four legs. Depending on the author, or storyteller, elves have ranged in size from being so small as to be nigh on invisible to having the same stature as humans. Elves have delighted in snaring humans in webs of magic and keeping them prisoner for thousands of years. Or they have lived quietly among the forests of the world, desiring only to be left alone to sing their songs and take delight in the plants and creatures of the woods.

However, no matter their size or their nature, one thing that has nearly always remained consistent about elves, regardless of who is describing them, is their association with all things magical and their ability to handle themselves during combat. Despite the fact that few elves have been depicted as delighting in war, there have been only a scant number who have been unable to master the tools of combat. A good thing, too, for since Tolkien made them part of the modern lexicon of fantastical beings with his epic sagas of their histories and sorrows (The Lord of the Rings and *The Silmarillion*), elves have appeared in story after story as a race beset by enemies and standing firm against the face of darkness everywhere. The elves are the ones who always seem to pay the heaviest price in any conflict. Most often, however, it seems that their deeds are ignored, unnoticed, or forgotten by humans, who have invaded their worlds with their noise and bustle.

Perhaps it is because the elves measure lives in centuries, and sometimes even millennia, and are willing to shoulder the responsibility for the mistakes they have made down through time that have led to armed conflict, they feel compelled to bear the heaviest strokes of an enemy army's swords as a type of penance. Or it could also be a simple matter of practicality, because as fighters they are invariably superior to the majority of the humans they end up allied with. Due to the incredible span of their years, they also have had the most time to amass reasons to seek vengeance, for their memories are as long as their years.

Arya: The Proud Princess

Despite the fact that elves are also known for their abilities as artists, creators of beautiful poetry and songs, and lovers of music, there is a noticeable lack of joy or levity among most races of elves that you are liable to come across in modern fantasy literature. Of course, if *you* had spent hundreds, if not thousands, of years in sporadic battles against the forces of darkness and seen many of your loved ones killed during them, some of the joy might have gone out of your life. In a great many stories that include elves, they are supplied with the means of leaving the world they occupy to travel back to their point of origin, usually across a sea, to a land where they will be able to forget the cares they have accumulated while living among mortals. In fact, in most stories, at the beginning of the tale, elves are relatively unknown to the mortals, for not only have their numbers dwindled as more and more have chosen to leave the cares of the world behind them, those who remain have retreated from day-to-day contact with humans. Often the elves have come to be viewed with suspicion by the majority of humans, if the humans even believe in them.

So it's not much of a surprise to find, in Christopher Paolini's Inheritance cycle, elves living a life similar to the one just described. That's not to say that, with his depiction of the race, he's simply copied what others have already done, but rather that he's drawn upon the folklore of elves. Of course, in order to make them unique to the world he's created, the author has added some characteristics and removed others, to make sure that the reader has no trouble distinguishing these elves from ones who have graced the pages of other books. For although they share things—such as grace and agility beyond that of humans, living somewhere else prior to coming to their current home, immortality, and the gradual alienation of their race from humans — unlike their brothers and sisters in other tales, these elves cannot travel to another land to forget their cares.

For better or worse, ever since the elves made peace with the dragons and united the two races through the bonds of dragon and Dragon Rider, their story has been irrevocably tied to the fate of Alagaësia. As Oromis tells Eragon, there was a time when the elves weren't immortal and didn't possess anywhere near the powers they have in the present. Although it's never made clear when the change took place, it could only have happened after the disappearance of the Grey Folk and the casting of the spell that turned the ancient language into the language of magic (*Eldest* p. 399). Perhaps it was because the elves adopted the language as their own that something about speaking it and nothing else imbued their beings with magic, transforming them into the way they were when Eragon met them. There is some logic in that, when you consider the transformation that Eragon began to undergo — even before he was completely changed and healed during the ceremony under the Menoa tree (*Eldest* p. 469) — because he was exposed to Saphira's magic.

Like the majority of mortals in Alagaësia, Eragon did not even believe that elves existed when Brom first told him about them. The first elf Eragon meets is Arya. His lack of experience with elves may be partly responsible for him being so besotted with her from the moment he lays eyes on her in the prison cell where Durza is holding her captive (*Eragon* p. 303). Nothing in his young life could have prepared him for her ethereal beauty. Of course, there's also nothing like a damsel in distress to spur romantic notions in the mind and heart of a young man who has had little contact with the opposite sex, let alone an elf whose beauty outstrips that of any mortal. However, it turns out that Eragon couldn't have picked someone any less appropriate to have a crush on if he had tried.

The elves were the first Dragon Riders. As such, the elves believe that they bear a great deal of the responsibility for not being able to withstand Galbatorix and the Forsworn when they set out on their spree of destruction, killing those Riders who were not of the Forsworn. But the fact is that the Riders had grown complacent and proud. Because of this, their enemies were able to pick them off individually. With each kill, the Forsworn amassed more power and gained more strength, until the Dragon Riders were no longer sufficient in power or numbers to withstand them. Since the final defeat of the Dragon Riders, the elves have been preparing themselves in case another Rider came into being who could be counted on to spearhead their effort to overthrow Galbatorix.

When Jeod and Brom were able to liberate one of the three eggs from the clutches of the king, there was reluctance on the part of both the elves and the human Varden to allow it to be the province of only one of the races. Although there were elves who didn't believe it was in the best interests of the world to allow another human to become the newest Rider, it was, after all, a human Rider who was responsible for the mess they were in. Therefore, it was decided that the egg was to spend equal time with each race, in order to allow it the best chance of hatching. Couriers were needed to carry the egg between the races, and only those who were totally dedicated to the task, who were willing to put everything else in their lives on hold, would do.

When Arya chose to become one of those dedicated few, the cost she paid was more than just risking her life for the cause; she risked her relationship with her mother, Islanzadí, the queen of the elves. Unbeknownst to any among the Varden, save Brom, Arya is the only daughter of the queen and heir to the throne of the elf kingdom. Yet because of her insistence upon serving as a courier for Saphira's egg, she and her mother have been estranged for seventy years, as we find out on Eragon's first visit to Ellesméra (*Eldest* pp. 226–227). Her mother had not wanted her to become a courier, and, in fact, had forbidden it. Thus it was in defiance of both her mother and her queen that Arya had dedicated herself to the task of trying to find the newest Dragon Rider. As a result, her mother had banned her from court and from her presence (*Eldest* p. 226). Yet when Islanzadí heard that her daughter had been captured while ferrying Saphira's egg, she assumed the worst—that she would die. Blaming the Varden for sending her daughter to her death, she cut off all relations with them and stopped all contact between her kingdom and the outer world, to the point of ceasing to scry with water or mirror to see what was transpiring beyond her borders (*Eldest* p. 268).

So despite the fact that Eragon sees Arya as someone to be wooed as a potential romantic partner, she sees in him the fulfillment of her hopes and dreams that one day the reign of Galbatorix will be overcome. After dedicating so much of her life to that goal, the idea that Eragon would allow anything, including being infatuated with her, to distract himself from his objective, is highly insulting to her. At one point, Oromis tries his best to explain Arya's situation to Eragon, so he can understand why his infatuation is so upsetting to her. He reminds Eragon that Eragon represents their best—indeed, their only—hope of overthrowing Galbatorix, and that even if he and Arya were suited for each other, she would not encourage a relationship between them because nothing must take precedence over being rid of the king (*Eldest* pp. 387–389).

We see Arya only through Eragon's eyes, and so our impressions of her character are formed by his limited vision. Upon her recovery from captivity, she becomes a leather-clad warrior maiden with ice in her veins. She dispatches Urgals with ease and, astride Saphira, calmly rides to Eragon's rescue in his battle with Durza (*Eragon* p. 490). The first chink appears in her armor when they are making the journey to Ellesméra for Eragon's training. After snapping at him for inquiring as to her state of mind, she confesses to him that she is frightened, although of what she doesn't say. Of course, we find out soon enough what she's frightened of; she's unsure of what reception awaits her from the queen, and maybe she's also unsure of her own feelings concerning her mother and whether she'll feel comfortable in what should be her home (*Eldest* pp. 163–164).

Once she is welcomed home by her mother, she appears to undergo something of a transformation and, on the surface, seems to be more relaxed. However, the more Eragon gets to know her, the more aware we become of what troubles her. Eragon seems quite adept at accidentally pushing her buttons, for upon discovering her status as princess and heir, he questions how she could have risked her life as a courier. She responds by angrily explaining the differences between human and elven princesses. Elven royalty are expected to do whatever is necessary for the good of the country, even if it means risking their own lives. If Arya had died while serving as ambassador to the Varden and the dwarves or while carrying out her courier duties, someone else would have been found to be successor to the throne. Anyway, if someone has no desire to rule, then nobody will make them do so; the elves do not wish to be led by someone who doesn't want to be a queen or king. As she is explaining this to Eragon, she gives him an unexpected peek into her inner thoughts as, almost to herself, she says that she had "many years to perfect those arguments with [her] mother" (*Eldest* p. 309). With those words, Arya could be referring to a lack of desire on her own part to be queen, but it's more likely that she's thinking back to the strife that had arisen between herself and her mother because of her choice to become a courier and ambassador.

Whatever the reason for those words, there is obviously still tension between mother and daughter, in spite of the apparent reconciliation between the two upon Arya's return. Arya was obviously hurt by her mother's treatment of her and still hasn't completely forgiven her. Arya remains mostly aloof from Eragon until *Brisingr*, obviously fearing that any softening on her part might encourage him to hope for a romantic involvement. She does begin to reveal more of herself during their travels together when she meets up with him after he kills the Ra'zac and helps rescue Katrina. Part of this is because Eragon has begun to show a little bit of wisdom in his dealings with her by respecting her wishes that he not mention anything more about romance and doing his best to treat her as a friend.

She still shows flashes of her old impatience with him when she has to explain why they have to make it look as though the soldiers they killed had been slain by weapons, not magic (*Brisingr* p. 186). It's moments such as these that make you realize the wide gulf that separates the two, and why there is so little chance of them becoming romantically involved, no matter how close they may become. True, she turns to Eragon for comfort when they find out about the deaths of Oromis and Glaedr, but it's only because circumstances have put them together at the moment, and he is someone who can understand what she is feeling at the time (*Brisingr* p. 739).

The truth of the matter is that even by the end of *Brisingr*, we know little about Arya, except for what Eragon has been able to glean directly from her. Observation tells us that she is strong-willed, even for an elf. She stood up to her mother for what she believed in. She withstood torture and questioning by Durza, a fearsome warrior and deadly sorcerer. And, of course, she is completely dedicated to the overthrow of Galbatorix.

As the only daughter of Islanzadí, queen of the elves, Arya stands to inherit the throne if she so desires, and although we have no indication as to her intentions, there are signs that suggest she would probably assume that mantle if she were called. Arya feels some resentment toward her mother because of her mother's refusal to give her blessing for Arya's desire to be an ambassador and courier. The fact that she did it anyway, despite knowing that it would damage her relationship with her mother, proves that she is able and willing to put the good of the whole ahead of her own individual needs, exactly what she told Eragon an elven monarch must do. In the coming war, I predict that Islanzadí will be killed and Arya will have to step into the breach. If her mother were to die during peacetime, perhaps Arya would turn down the throne. But if her mother were to die during a war, Arya would not desert the elves in their hour of need. The death of the queen, combined with the recent loss of Oromis and Glaedr, would leave the elves devastated and create a void that would need to be filled as quickly as possible.

If Arya were to refuse to become queen, the gap in leadership and the ensuing chaos could very well doom the elves. Galbatorix would take advantage of the elvish turmoil by attacking them with as much force as possible in the hope of destroying them. Only if Arya assumed command immediately and provided leadership could that be prevented. If she becomes queen, it's doubtful that she will surrender that position, for she will be needed after the war almost as much as she was during it, to help lead the elves into whatever the new age holds for them. As the individual among the elves who has been most actively involved in working to restore the Dragon Riders, and the one most familiar with events and personalities in the outside world, she will be ideally suited for helping the elves establish themselves on an equal footing with everybody else.

Although it's true that Eragon and Saphira will most likely end up living among the elves as they become the teachers of all future dragons and their Riders—with Glaedr's help, of course—they, like all previous Riders, will remain independent from the throne. This will apply to Eragon's personal relationship with Arya as well, for no matter what either of them may feel by that time, I doubt the elves would allow a human to be their king. Anyway, as a Dragon Rider, Eragon wouldn't be able to rule over any one people, as Riders are meant to act as overseers of all the rulers to ensure the well-being of every citizen of Alagaësia and beyond.

Hopefully, in Book Four Paolini will allow us to get to know Arya a little better, perhaps even see the world through her eyes. However, whether we do or not, it won't make any difference regarding what becomes of her. She won't be able to deny the call of her heritage and birthright and will ascend to the throne as queen of the elves. Whatever the future holds for the elves, Arya will be the one to lead them into it.

Chapter 7

Nasuada: The Lady of the Varden

For far too long, the complexion of fantasy has been almost exclusively pale. Heroes of either gender have been fair with steely gray eyes and dark hair, or with flaxen locks and sea blue eyes. Rarely do you meet a hero with ebony skin and brown eyes. Although the days of Tolkien's "swarthy men" filling the ranks of enemy armies are a thing of the past, villainy and evil are still associated predominantly with the color black, while the forces of good are far too often the golden-haired boys and girls. It would be best if the color of a character's skin didn't matter much, so that it wasn't a characteristic necessarily even described, but it's also unrealistic to expect that, when the world we live in is far from color-blind. The best we can hope for is that authors make an attempt to have their characters be as representative of the real world as possible, and that we break free of the old white equals good, black equals bad mind-set that has dominated fantasy for so long.

The Inheritance cycle proves how easy it is to do this. Christopher Paolini gracefully includes the characters of Ajihad, the leader of the Varden when Eragon first joins them, and his daughter and successor, Nasuada. Despite the fact that black-skinned people seem to form a minority of Alagaësia's population, remember Roran's question after meeting Nasuada about whether she dyed her skin (*Eldest* p. 663). Their physical appearance isn't an issue, it's just a fact of life. The question of their heritage is something of a mystery until *Brisingr*, when we are introduced to other members of Nasuada and her father's tribe (*Brisingr* p. 95). Even then, we don't learn that much about them except for a few details, such as they are skilled in the working of gold and silver and, although some of their people live in the cities, an equal number still live as nomads in tribal groups. As the visit wasn't merely a social call, we also find out about certain tribal rituals used to determine leadership (*Brisingr* p. 100).

However, that's jumping ahead in Nasuada's story, and it would be best to start with how Eragon first gets to know her in *Eldest*. For although we first meet her in *Eragon* (p. 449), at the time she's a minor character, the daughter of the leader of the Varden, described only as being a couple of years older than Eragon and strikingly beautiful. In fact, Murtagh, upon meeting her, comments that she has more grace and style than any of the noblewomen whom he used to see in Galbatorix's court, so elegant and noble is her appearance and bearing (*Eragon* p. 465). However, it's not until her father, Ajihad, is killed in the same raid that sees Murtagh captured by Urgals (*Eldest* p. 6) that Eragon and the reader really begin to get to know and appreciate Nasuada.

Almost immediately, the impression we receive of her is of a person far wiser than her years and one who is infinitely better prepared to lead the Varden into battle than anybody else. For although the Council of Elders, a group of people chosen by the population of the Varden at large to represent their interests with whomever leads the organization, tries to create a situation in which Nasuada would merely be a puppet to do their bidding, she slyly outmaneuvers them. She accepts Eragon's oath of loyalty to her individually instead of to the Varden in general, and then asks him to repeat it publicly when the council expects him to vow his oath of fidelity to the Varden (*Eldest* p. 24).

Due to his popularity, and the respect he's held in by the rest of the Varden, this makes it impossible for the council to gainsay any of her decisions without appearing to go against Eragon. It also means that she's the only one who can command him to do anything, as he is her personal subject. This wasn't a step that Eragon took lightly, for if Nasuada proved to be a bad leader, or power hungry, it could bind him to doing things he doesn't want to do. It also means that he can never publicly disobey or argue with her, because his stature is such among the Varden that if he does, he will have so undermined her authority that he might as well take her place as leader. Due to the fact that most of the time what's in the best interests of Eragon is in the best interests of the Varden, this becomes an issue only once, when Nasuada demands that he attend the gathering of the dwarf clans as her ambassador when they meet to choose their new king after the death of Hrothgar. Fortunately, when Eragon threatens to sulk, a wiser head— Saphira's—prevails, and he eventually agrees to Nasuada's demand (*Brisingr* p. 365).

It's of vital importance that the dwarves continue to support the Varden, after all, and if they were to elect a king from one of the clans who don't support the war, not only would the Varden lose half their fighting force without the dwarves' army, they would lose a valuable source of supplies and materials. Eragon is a good choice as ambassador, not only because of his standing as a Dragon Rider, but also because he is an adopted member of the same clan that Hrothgar used to lead, which can only increase the influence he will wield during the gathering. When it ends up that the dwarves do select a new king who supports the war, and Eragon plays a key role in ensuring that outcome, Nasuada's decision to send him turns out to have been the right one, no matter what Eragon might have thought. A leader has to consider everything in terms of the big picture, even if that means going against the wishes of as important an individual as Eragon. And a leader must be strong enough not to back down in the face of opposition. It is very lonely sometimes to be a leader, as you can't really have any close relationships among those who serve you; you never know when you might have to order them to do something they won't like doing.

Nasuada's importance as a character in the Inheritance cycle becomes apparent in *Eldest*, not only because of her status as leader of the Varden, but also because, aside from

Eragon and Roran, she is the only character to tell the story from her point of view. It's while Eragon is off training with elves that Paolini starts this process (*Eldest* p. 311), and not only do we learn about her in this manner, but it's how we are first introduced to Elva (*Eldest* p. 332). Although that might not seem like a big thing, it does mean that we are given access to her thoughts and her opinions instead of merely seeing her through the eyes of another character, as is the case with Arya and Murtagh. When an author goes to that much trouble with a character, it means that we really should be taking notice of all that's going on with the person in question.

Naturally, Nasuada is preoccupied with matters concerning the Varden and how to ensure their survival. The first step she takes as leader is to move them from their sanctuary in the dwarf kingdom to the country adjacent to Alagaësia, Surda. It may seem as though she's retreating from Galbatorix, but the truth of the matter is that the move puts the Varden in a better position to begin taking the attack to the Empire, rather than merely maintaining a defensive position. Anyway, now that the Empire has discovered the whereabouts of the hidden city of Trojheim, its use as a defensive fortification has been diminished, and the Varden's continued presence there places their hosts, the dwarves, at risk. Instead of risking her alliance with the dwarves by giving dissenting clans within the dwarf population reasons for ending the dwarf association with the Varden—it would be easy for those opposing the alliance to make arguments like "They're putting us at risk by their presence" or "If it weren't for them, the Empire wouldn't be attacking us"—by moving the Varden Nasuada has relieved King Hrothgar of having to answer questions and will help him maintain peace among the clans. In addition, she has given her people the opportunity to be in a position to fight back.

By seeing the world through her eyes, the reader quickly realizes that Nasuada doesn't take any steps lightly, even though she appears to make decisions quickly. She has such a firm grasp of the situation she is in, and such a complete understanding of the people who serve under her, that she is able to assess any new situation and circumstances swiftly while keeping in mind both the short-term and the long-term implications of her decisions. Of course, it doesn't hurt that she's the sole voice of authority and doesn't have to spend any time convincing others that her way is the right way. It looks, for example, as if she makes the decision to allow the Urgals to join their forces with the Varden (*Eldest* p. 609) without giving the matter much thought, because she comes to what appears to be a snap decision, disagreeing with her advisers. However, she knows very well that in the short term there are going to be problems among the three species (dwarf, human, and Urgal) in her army, but she also knows that once battle is joined against the forces of Galbatorix, the common enemy will unite them. She also guesses, rightly, that the dwarves and humans will be grateful that they are no longer facing the Urgals as enemies on the field of battle when they see the kind of damage they inflict upon the king's forces.

She is farsighted enough to realize that there will come a time when the whole question of what to do about the Urgals must be answered. For if the Varden are successful in their campaign to overthrow Galbatorix, the Urgals will still exist. It will be better to deal with them as allies after the war than as vanquished foes. She's not naive enough to believe that years of hatred on both sides can be set aside merely because the three species served together. Nor is she ignorant of the Urgals' social structure, which demands that males prove themselves in battle in order to secure status and mates, and is therefore aware that she may have set forth on a course that can't be resolved. Yet there is the hope that continued interaction among the three races will help to teach each of them enough about the other that they will come to respect the other for their abilities and courage and thus be able to coexist peacefully. It's for this reason that she places Roran in charge of the first mixed patrol party of Urgals and humans that she sends out, knowing full well that an Urgal will most likely challenge his authority. Of all her captains, Roran is the only one who will not only be able to handle the situation physically, but deal with the aftermath in such a way as to ensure a positive outcome.

Yet Nasuada is more than just a leader. She's a person with fears and regrets, and even though she has schooled herself to hide them from the rest of the world, she's honest enough with herself that she neither denies their existence nor lets them rule her. If you're wondering what she has to be afraid of, aside from the obvious stuff—being assassinated or making a decision that results in disaster for the Varden—try to put yourself in her shoes for a second. Here you are, maybe nineteen years old, a woman, surrounded by men twice your age and who knows how many times stronger and more experienced in battle than you are, and yet *you're* giving *them* orders. Despite the fact that she was the designated heir of her father, and was appointed to the task by the council, she would still have to deal with, and overcome, the intimidation she must be feeling at being thrust into this type of situation. That she's also expected to act as judge for all the petty disputes bound to arise among people forced to live together in cramped conditions means that her word has to be accepted as absolute authority by everybody in the Varden. Sometimes it must be difficult for her to figure out whether she is sitting in judgment of them or, with the amount of scrutiny she's under, the reverse.

To maintain order, Nasuada must take a hard line on any transgression, no matter what the circumstances. She is forced to have Roran whipped when he disobeys his captain's orders on a raiding mission against the Empire, even though his doing so saved the lives of everybody in the raiding party, including that of the captain (*Brisingr* pp. 516–527). However, because the captain presses charges against Roran (the captain is an officious and incompetent idiot who doesn't like to be shown up), she has no choice but to have him whipped for disobeying a superior officer's direct order while in battle. This discipline is meted out to ensure that her authority is seen as absolute and that nobody is allowed to get away with breaking the laws that govern the Varden (*Brisingr* p. 568). But then Nasuada demotes the captain, bends the rules of the punishment and allows Roran to be healed from the whipping, and then promotes him to replace the man who had arrested him

(*Brisingr* p. 577). In this way, she ensures that the letter of the law is carried out and justice is served as well.

To know one's own fears and overcome them is bravery of the highest order. Time and time again, Nasuada overcomes her fears to do what is required for her to both lead and remain leader of the Varden. Whether it's facing down members of her own tribe who challenge her right to lead or making the decision to force Galbatorix's hand by attacking him instead of waiting to be attacked, time after time she proves herself more than capable of doing what's necessary. We know that she is right to accept the test of her leadership offered by her fellow tribal members in the Trial of the Long Knives, in which each participant cuts himself or herself on the arm until one retires or passes out from loss of blood (*Brisingr* pp. 100–107). For when she defeats him, she ensures the full support of the tribes for the Varden. In addition, the Trial of the Long Knives also further cements her place as rightful ruler of the Varden in the minds of her own people by showing her strength of purpose and her lack of fear.

As for her decision to take the war to Galbatorix, although her forces have had an initial victory at the end of *Brisingr*, whether it was the correct thing to do is still to be determined, as is the fate of all Alagaësia. However, swiftly by forcing Galbatorix to take to the field against two armies — the elves in the north and the combined armies of the Varden, the dwarves, the Urgals, and Surda in the south — she is ensuring that he's forced to concentrate on battles instead of trying to hatch the final egg, or finding other ways that he can increase his magical advantage.

Nasuada: The Lady of the Varden

With her authority assured, Nasuada has to be considered one of the most powerful people on the continent by the time the reader reaches *Brisingr*. Not only does she have a Dragon Rider at her command, but she also controls one of the largest armed forces in the region. Aside from Eragon, she's probably the person whom Galbatorix—as the assassination attempts prove (*Eldest* pp. 518-519)—worries about the most as an opponent because of the authority she possesses. Yet in spite of her position, she's not without regrets. And no matter how much she tells herself that she has plenty to be proud of, and that few others could have done what she's done, that doesn't prevent her from feeling that there's something missing from her life when she meets Katrina and sees how much Roran loves her (*Brisingr* p. 122).

Nasuada has spent virtually her entire life among the Varden (*Eragon* p. 453), according to Orik, Eragon's friend and Hrothgar's successor as king of the dwarves. She came to the Varden with her father when she was an infant, and a good deal of her time has been devoted to being groomed by her father to take over in the event of his death. So she's never had the chance to experience any of the things most people her age take for granted, such as confiding in friends, falling in love, or considering marriage in any terms except those of political expediency or advantage. She can't afford to say the wrong word ever, show a moment's weakness, or be subject to any of the frailties of emotion that other humans, no matter what their age or status, are given the freedom to wallow in. Nasuada is so wrapped up in being a leader and considering people as assets and how she can best use them, either in battle or to maintain her position, that she rarely considers them in any other light. So she is shocked to discover that while Eragon is away with Roran rescuing Katrina, she misses Eragon personally, not just because he is a Dragon Rider (*Brisingr* p. 118). But as anyone who remembers her spontaneous embrace of Eragon after she discovers he's alive, following his first battle with Murtagh (*Eldest* p. 660), might suspect, she harbors feelings for him that are deeper than those normally held by a liege lord for her servant.

The author has been deliberate in everything he's done so far in the Inheritance cycle, so letting us see all these aspects of Nasuada's character has been done for a reason. Later on, I'll look at her specifically in light of her potential as both a Dragon Rider and as a love interest for Eragon. However, I introduce both topics here in the hope that a detailed examination of her character will help substantiate the arguments I make about her later in this book.

That she has feelings for Eragon that are deeper than even she is willing to admit is becoming evident by the way she treats him and her reactions to him when she allows her guard to slip, even for a moment. As far as what will happen after the war when it comes to her holding a position of power, well, if the Dragon Riders assume their old role of overseeing the various rulers and ensuring that nobody is taking advantage of anybody else, can you see anybody more suited to the job of Dragon Rider than Nasuada? She is respected by the Urgals for being the first human leader in history to establish real relationships with them, and she is esteemed by the other three species for her bravery, intelligence, and fairness. Time and again, she has proven herself willing to make sacrifices in order to ensure harmony among her followers, and has also shown that she's willing to make the difficult and unpopular decisions required of an unbiased arbitrator. So aside from all the other characteristics she possesses that make her an ideal candidate for being a Dragon Rider, of all the other possible Riders, she is the one most suited to assume the role the Riders of old played for Alagaësia and the continent.

As things stand right now, it looks as though Galbatorix will have to be defeated for the last dragon egg to hatch for any of the likely candidates, Roran, Arya, and Nasuada. It doesn't seem possible for there to be any other way that anyone could ever lay hands on it. (Of course, there's always the chance of something unlikely happening, such as Murtagh attempting to redeem himself by stealing the egg and although he is success-ful in carrying it to the Varden, he is so severely wounded that he dies and Thorn follows shortly thereafter, but not before bequeathing his Eldunarí to Eragon. But it is to be hoped that Paolini doesn't allow that to happen, for not only would it stretch credulity to the breaking point, this Hollywood cliché would ruin the realism that he has created in the story.) Once the war is over, Nasuada's role as leader of the Varden will become redundant, and even if it weren't, it's highly doubt-ful that she'd want to continue on in the position anyway. The task she set for herself was to overthrow Galbatorix — to "oversee the birth of a new age" (*Brisingr* p. 122), as she puts it — and what better way to continue doing that than as a Dragon Rider? Of course, it's not her decision, but should the opportunity arise, there'd be no doubting either the aptness of her selection or her ability to become a Dragon Rider.

As a Rider, the last obstacle standing between her and Eragon becoming a couple would be set aside, as she would now be as immortal as him. And once her training was completed, they could marry. In fact, with the two Riders being connected so strongly, it would only make matters easier for Saphira to mate with Nasuada's dragon, as they couldn't help but be affected by the bond between their Riders. It would really be a happily-ever-after of the best kind if the four of them could retire to the relative peace of Ellesméra and begin the process of repopulating the world with dragons and Dragon Riders.

The Lady Nasuada is a remarkable person who has been forced to draw upon every ounce of courage and resourcefulness at her disposal in order to ensure the survival of the Varden, and to cement her position as its leader. I predict that she will fulfill her goal of ushering in a new age of peace and glory for Alagaësia, as well as for all the countries and people surrounding it. Although Eragon might be the point at the end of the spear that will finally pierce Galbatorix's heart, it is Nasuada's hands that are guiding the spear home. Once it is lodged firmly in place, it will be her turn to take flight in the skies above the land she fought for and continue to offer its people her wisdom and leadership skills, if from a slightly different perspective.

Chapter 8

For Whom the Egg Hatches

*"The Varden and the Empire aren't fighting to con-
trol this land or its people. Their goal is to control
the next generation of Riders, of whom you are the
first. Whoever controls these Riders will become
the undisputed master of Alagaësia....Even though
the Riders are gone, there are still three dragon
eggs left – all of them in Galbatorix's possession.
Actually there are only two now, since Saphira
hatched. The king salvaged the three during his last
great battle with the Riders....He has the remaining
two guarded so thoroughly that it would be suicide
to try and steal them." (Eragon pp. 224–226)*

And now there is one. Before Saphira hatched, there were
three dragon eggs, representing the future population of dragons in Alagaësia. Now there is only one left. For at the end of

Eldest, it was revealed that Galbatorix had taken control of Murtagh by learning his true name. Then he had taken him to the remaining two dragon eggs, and one of them hatched for him into the red dragon known as Thorn. In their first meeting, aided by the power of Galbatorix, Murtagh and Thorn easily defeated Eragon and Saphira. Murtagh only released them when he found a loophole in Galbatorix's instructions to himself that allowed him to disobey the king without risk (*Eldest* pp. 651–652). Their second battle was much closer, as Eragon was able to draw upon twelve elvish spellcasters and Arya for enough power to battle Murtagh to a draw (*Brisingr* pp. 317–329).

With the discovery that Murtagh's power probably rests in his use of a dragon's heart of hearts, and with Eragon coming into possession of one of his own at the end of *Brisingr*, the balance of power between the two sides—the Empire and the Varden—in terms of Dragon Riders is once again even. Of course, Galbatorix himself could enter the fray and tip the balance to the Empire. But so far he seems loath to do so, except when Murtagh and Thorn looked ready to fall before Oromis and Glaedr (*Brisingr* p. 731). In fact, up to that point he was more concerned with capturing Eragon and Saphira alive and turning them to his cause—probably by the same means that he used on Murtagh—than actually fighting them.

All of which makes the person whom the third egg chooses to hatch for all the more crucial. If Galbatorix is able to find another individual whom he can control and whom the remaining egg will hatch for, the scales will tip so far in his favor that the Varden and Eragon would have little hope of ever overthrowing him. Although Glaedr's heart of hearts might supply Eragon with sufficient power to defeat Murtagh, it's doubtful he and Saphira would be able to withstand a concentrated attack on them by two Riders whose powers have been augmented by Galbatorix. Of course, the Varden are at a large disadvantage in this matter, as Galbatorix isn't liable to start inviting their potential Dragon Riders to drop in and try their luck with getting the egg to hatch. Somehow or other, they are going to have to steal the egg back, or the question of whom it will hatch for will become moot.

Keeping It in the Family: Roran

So far, the first two eggs have hatched to members of the same family—the half-brothers Murtagh and Eragon, who have the same mother. Therefore, it's only logical to assume that there is something in their bloodline that speaks to dragons. Following that line of thinking, the most obvious candidate available to have the last egg hatch for him would be Roran, Eragon and Murtagh's cousin through their mother.

On the surface, he would seem to be ideal. He is a proven warrior and fearsome in his opposition to and hatred of everything that Galbatorix and the Empire stand for. However, there are reasons to believe that he would have hesitations about being a Dragon Rider, and there's no way the dragon egg could fail to pick up on those feelings. Think of all he went through to rescue Katrina; would a man who convinced an entire village of people to cross the country in order to put himself in the position where he could save the woman he loved give up that relationship for anything?

If Roran were to become a Dragon Rider, he would become virtually immortal, which would mean he would be faced with the prospect of watching Katrina grow old and die while he stayed young. I can't see him even considering that sort of life, can you? Sure, he's fascinated by magic and tries to speak the words that will move a stone, but he shows little affinity for it and so far hasn't had any luck in casting that simple spell. Now, of course, if he were partnered with a dragon, things would be different, as abilities that had lain dormant could very well be awoken, but it really doesn't seem likely.

For there's also Roran's character to consider. Compare him with both of his cousins, and you'll see a world of difference. When we first meet Roran, he doesn't have any ambitions beyond marrying Katrina, setting himself up with some land, and raising a family, just like his father did (*Eragon* p. 57). He's so down to earth, so practical — so human, if you will — that it almost seems that it would go against his nature to be a Dragon Rider.

Despite the fact that we don't see into Murtagh's head in quite the same way that we do with Eragon, it's obvious that he and his half-brother share characteristics that Roran lacks that helped them to make a connection with their eggs/dragons. Eragon, especially, is shown to be far more fanciful than Roran; he was captivated by Brom's tales long before he came into possession of the dragon egg. Can you picture either Eragon or Murtagh as ever having been content to be farmers or settle down to a quiet family life?

Something else that's important to remember is that both Eragon and Murtagh grew up as outsiders. Neither of them was raised by his parents. In Murtagh's case, he was badly abused by his father when he was young. And both have experienced the sense of being different from others. Although Eragon's childhood was nowhere near as awful as Murtagh's, he still went through his early years known as Sone of None, and both of them would have grown up yearning for something to fill the void that being an orphan would have caused. Even if they couldn't have articulated it, both of them were unconsciously looking for the type of companionship that being a Dragon Rider would offer, and that's bound to have been something that their dragons would have picked up on.

Roran, on the other hand, was an accepted member of the community in which he and Eragon had grown up. As the eldest son, he stood to inherit his father's farm, giving him a sense of place and purpose that his cousins lacked. If circumstances had allowed, I doubt that he would have left his valley for any reason. It was only because he wasn't given any choice in the matter that he has done the things he's done to this point. Extraordinary circumstances can turn the ordinary into extraordinary, and that's what has happened to Roran. Almost everything he's done has been against his natural inclinations. When the war is over, he will probably be more than content to be a farmer and raise a family with Katrina, as he had planned all along—and that would be difficult to do if he were a Dragon Rider.

Although Roran has developed into a fearsome warrior and a strong leader of humans and Urgals, he lacks many of the intangibles that both Murtagh and Eragon possess that would make him a viable candidate as the match for the final egg. Even if he were offered the opportunity to be a Dragon Rider, although he might be tempted, he would never abandon Katrina. We need to look elsewhere for the person who will be a match for the third egg.

What About an Elf? Arya

The elves were the first creatures to forge an alliance with the dragons and they were the first Dragon Riders, so it is only natural to consider the possibility of the egg hatching for one of them. Although it's true that there was plenty of opportunity for Saphira to have hatched for an elf when her egg was with them, that doesn't mean that there isn't an elf who's suited to be a Dragon Rider. It just means that Saphira and Eragon were destined for each other. Now, although there are plenty of elves — and we've even met a couple who initially resented the fact that Eragon, a human, became a Dragon Rider — the one who springs to mind as the potential match for the final egg is, of course, Arya.

She has the knowledge, the ability, and the courage to be an incredible Dragon Rider, as she has shown herself able to stand up to anything that Galbatorix has thrown at her. Not only did she survive the ordeal of being imprisoned by Durza the Shade (*Eragon* p. 303), she, like Eragon, was able to kill a Shade without suffering any permanent damage, physically or emotionally (*Brisingr* p. 738). On top of that, she spent many years acting as the courier for Saphira's egg, carrying it back and forth between the Varden and the elves. Even when she was captured, she had the presence of mind to attempt to send the egg to Brom, so that it would stay out of the hands of the enemy (*Eragon* p. 4).

So great was her dedication to the fight against Galbatorix that she even defied her mother, the queen of the elves, in order to carry out her duties to the cause. Like Eragon and Murtagh, she knows what it's like to be an outsider, as she spent seventy years estranged from her mother because of her decision to help the Varden. When she escorts Eragon to the homeland of the elves in *Eldest*, so that he can continue his training, it marks the first time in seventy years that she's been home. It seems that the characteristics of being an outsider—the things that set you apart from the rest of your community—play a major role in dictating who becomes a Dragon Rider. Independence and self-reliance are things that Murtagh, Eragon, Arya, and even Galbatorix have in common, and each of them developed those characteristics from having to do things on their own, or because they've never quite felt that they belonged anywhere. Look at how uncomfortable Arya is when she is first back home in Ellesméra. In fact, one gets the feeling that it's almost a relief for her to be able to leave the city, and the kingdom, and return to the Varden.

However, the fact remains that she is heir to the throne of the elven kingdom, and she will accept her responsibilities and become queen of the elves when the need arises. Being queen would preclude her from being a Dragon Rider, because she would have to be concerned with the specific interests of one people, while a Dragon Rider has to represent all the free races—dwarves, humans, Urgals, and elves—in battle and in peace. As with Roran, Arya has, shall we say, a previous commitment, something else that exerts a claim on her sense of duty. Just the chance that she might one day become queen would be enough of a reason for her to not be chosen by the last egg. Unless a person is completely without attachments, they do not have the singularity of focus that's required for the job of Dragon Rider.

If Not Them, Who? Nasuada?

When her father, Ajihad, was killed at the beginning of *Eldest* (p. 6), Nasuada assumed the leadership of the Varden. Although young, she had been groomed by her father to replace him in the event of his death, and so she was fully prepared when the Council of Elders tried to turn her into a figurehead. She's brave, smart, and willing to do whatever is necessary to defeat the Empire. Like Eragon and Murtagh, she grew up learning how to be independent and self-reliant, as her mother is dead and her father was busy with the job of leading the resistance against Galbatorix. Although she wasn't an outsider in the same way that the two half-brothers were, she still must have grown up somewhat isolated from the rest of her community because of her status as the daughter of the leader, and the training she went through to prepare her to be his heir.

She is now committed to leading the Varden, but what will happen after the war? With the chances of the final egg hatching while the war is on being very low and Nasuada's responsibilities as leader of the Varden done with, she'll have no other commitments stealing her focus. True, there's always the option that she could become one of the rulers of Alagaësia, but history has shown us that there have been plenty of times that the people who have led revolutions haven't been the best suited to being peacetime rulers. Once they have experienced the excitement of leading armies and planning battles, the mundane day-to-day running of a country doesn't appeal to them.

Admittedly, Nasuada is a long shot for becoming the last Dragon Rider of this generation, but she can't be discounted either. The way it stands now, anyway, all of the potential candidates are long shots for, as the quote at the beginning of this chapter reminds us, Galbatorix is in possession of the two remaining eggs. Of course, there's always the chance that the Varden will decide that it's worth the risk and attempt to steal the last egg, but that would seriously endanger at least one main character, probably Roran, as he would most likely lead the skirmish.

Of course, that does leave open an interesting scenario: Roran leads a raid into Galbatorix's stronghold to snatch the final dragon egg and, during the raid, the egg hatches for him. He's then captured by Galbatorix, who compels him to be his servant by the same means he has used to control Murtagh. I know, that's a little far-fetched, but it would make an interesting plot twist, although one that I think Christopher Paolini would have a hard time working his way through in the final book.

Or Nobody?

There's also one final option: the egg doesn't hatch for any of the existing characters. In some ways, this would be the easiest for Paolini to manage, as he wouldn't have to devote huge swathes of the book to stealing it and could concentrate instead on having Eragon figure out how he's going to separate Galbatorix from his stash of hearts of hearts. Isn't it more important to defeat the Empire than to secure the final egg? It won't really matter how many eggs or Riders the Varden have, if none of them are able to defeat Galbatorix. Think about what Eragon has had to go through to learn what he knows. Consider the fact that both of the people who taught him are dead. How could anybody who has the egg hatch for them, if they aren't part of the Empire, seriously hope to be of any use in the upcoming war, with no teachers and so little time to prepare?

Not only is there no one available who could provide the kind of training that Eragon received, there's no time for anyone to be trained. The Varden have started to take the battle to the Empire now, and in between fighting and searching for the means to defeat Galbatorix, even if Eragon were able to train a new Rider, he wouldn't have the time or the energy. In fact, having the third egg hatch could even present a danger for the Varden, as it would give Galbatorix a chance to capture whoever it is and turn that person, just as he turned Murtagh.

Sure, there's the chance that the egg could hatch for Arya, and she'd need far less training than anybody else to become a Dragon Rider, but the dragon would still need time to mature. The only reason that Thorn is ready for fighting now is the fact that Galbatorix has used magic to speed his growth. Even if anybody among the Varden or the elves were capable of casting that type of spell, they would never consider doing that to a dragon, for fear of the long-term damage it could cause the dragon. So even if an egg were to hatch for one of "the Good Guys" in Book Four, it wouldn't accomplish anything, except to give them something else they'd have to worry about.

The final egg is a symbol of what both sides are fighting for: the power to shape and control the nature of future Dragon Riders. If Eragon, the Varden, the elves, and the dwarves win in the end, the egg will represent the first step along a path that will return them to the glory days of Alagaësia, when Riders and their dragons helped the people prosper and kept the country safe. In some ways, the whole issue of the third egg hatching is a red herring, as it won't have any bearing on the present conflict, and it won't hatch until after the war is over.

The reality is that there have been only two characters we've met in the series so far who've had the qualifications to become a Dragon Rider. And both Eragon and Murtagh have had an egg hatch for them. Although Roran, Arya, and Nasuada each has characteristics and abilities that are needed by a Dragon Rider, each of them falls short in one way or another. When that's combined with the fact that a new Rider for the Varden would be of little use at this point, it only makes sense that the egg will not hatch until sometime in the unforeseeable future. If all that is hoped for comes to pass, this will mark the first in a long line of a new breed of Dragon Riders, representing all the free peoples of Alagaësia and the return of a golden age.

Chapter 9

What's in a Name?

As we've learned, in Alagaësia there's lots in a name. First of all, the whole system of magic is predicated on knowing something's name. In order to cast a spell, you have to be able to first define, in the ancient language, what it is you want to do. In *Eldest*, Oromis explains how the Grey Folk, a mysterious people who were around long before the elves were immortal, were the first people to control magic. They did so by casting a spell that gave the ancient language control over the magic that, until that time, had run wild throughout the world. Since that time, a knowledge of the ancient language has been a prerequisite for being a spellcaster (*Eldest* p. 399).

Knowing the name of, or the words that describe, an object, a person, or an element, allows a person to exert control over it. By stringing together a series of words that both define an object and what you want it—the object—to do, a person can make something do what they want, as long as they have the energy to power a spell. Of course, you have to be *exactly* sure of the meaning or, as Eragon discovered when he thought he was blessing Elva and ended up cursing her, you can have a full-scale disaster on your hands (*Eldest* pp. 294–295). Intent, what you want to do and whether you mean good or harm, has no effect on the spell if you've used the wrong word or changed the meaning of the word by using it in the wrong context.

The main reason that the Grey Folk devised this method was to ensure that there would be a measure of control exerted over the magic. A person could therefore be distracted from their intent—say, starting a fire—and not accidentally set their whistling neighbor jogging by who caught their eye and diverted their attention, on fire. As well as giving the ancient language the power to control magic, the Grey Folk also gave it two other characteristics: (1) nobody can lie while speaking it; and (2) it has "the ability to describe the true nature of things" (*Eldest* p. 399). The former is useful for ensuring that someone swearing an oath will keep it, and the latter is, of course, how the ancient language is used for casting spells.

The other important thing to realize about the ancient language and its ability to control magic and names, is that nothing need be said aloud. As Oromis explains to Eragon, most spellcasters say their spells aloud as it allows them a means of focusing their thoughts, but it is possible to simply think a spell for it to work (*Eldest* p. 398). The difficulty with this approach is that you have to be very careful not to be distracted while doing this, or you could set your neighbor on fire!

Now, in the same way that knowing the true name of a thing allows one to control it, knowing a person's true name — the description of their true nature — in the ancient language allows a person to control another person. On the surface, that might sound easy — learn somebody's name and presto! You can make them do anything you want. However, think about it for a second, and you'll begin to understand how difficult it really is to learn somebody's true name. Listen to the process that Christopher Paolini has Eragon go through when he discovers Sloan's true name:

> ...he had isolated the core elements of Sloan's personality, those things one could not remove without irrevocably changing the man. There occurred to him, then, three words in the ancient language that seemed to embody Sloan, and without thinking about it, Eragon whispered the words under his breath.... [H]e had, quite by accident, chanced upon Sloan's true name. (Brisingr pp. 79–80)

After Eragon and Roran had rescued Katrina from the grasp of the Ra'zac at the beginning of Brisingr, Eragon hid from the others the fact that Katrina's father, Sloan, whose betrayal of the villagers had led to Katrina's capture, was still alive (Brisingr p. 56). He knew that if Sloan were taken back to the Varden, he would certainly be killed for his treachery. His execution would devastate Katrina. And he didn't think that she would have been able to forgive any of those, including Roran, responsible for his execution. So instead of risking Katrina and Roran's relationship, he had Saphira fly Roran and Katrina back to the Varden while he stayed behind to ensure that the Ra'zac were truly defeated. In reality, he needed them out of the way so he could devise a means of dealing with Sloan other than killing him (*Brisingr* p. 62).

In an effort to figure out what to do with Sloan, Eragon allowed himself to think back over everything he knew about Sloan from when he had known him as the butcher in his hometown. To that, he added all the other information people had told him about Sloan's life that made him the person he was. It was only after he had taken the time to trace all the connections between the events and the emotions of Sloan's life that he "wove a tangled web, the patterns of which represented who Sloan was" and "he finally comprehended the reasons for Sloan's behavior" (*Brisingr* p. 79). Even though Sloan wasn't the most complicated of men, and was someone with whom Eragon was very familiar, it was still only by accident that he was able to figure out the three words in the ancient language that described his true nature and that, taken together, made up his true name.

Can you imagine how difficult it would be to figure out the true name of someone as complicated as Galbatorix? Or even worse, someone whom you didn't know well at all? If you want to give yourself an idea of the difficulties involved, think of someone you know really well—your best friend, or maybe your brother or sister—and now try to come up with the words that describe their true nature. Where it gets really tricky is figuring out what exactly is meant by the words *true nature*. It's more than just a person's characteristics, such as being hot-tempered or being friendly. Think of the person in the same way that you would an element, such as fire. How would you describe its true nature? Now make that a name.

Unlike the ancient language, most human languages don't have the capacity for naming in that sense, which makes it hard for us to even understand the concept. We normally have names that signify something through association not function, let alone its real nature. Think about a common object around the house, such as a chair. Aside from the fact that you know a chair is that object you sit on, what does the word actually tell you about it? What does that word have to do with describing an object whose function is to support a human body in a semiupright position? Can you think of any words that might describe the who and what of that object in such a way that somebody who didn't know what it was would understand its purpose without seeing it? If you can do that, you're beginning to understand just what a complex thing it is to come up with a person's true name.

At the end of *Eldest*, Murtagh reveals that Galbatorix is controlling Thorn and himself through his knowledge of their true names (*Eldest* p. 650). At the time, the only solution that Eragon can offer him as an alternative to being a slave, forced to murder people in the name of the Empire, is for Murtagh to allow Eragon to kill him. It's only natural that Murtagh would resist this suggestion; to be honest, can you blame him? If you were in his position, would you think it such a hot idea? He's young, he's powerful, and he loves Thorn—remember, if a Dragon Rider dies, so does his or her dragon—so the idea of sacrificing his own life so that others might live can't seem like a fair exchange (*Eldest* p. 650).

It's only at their second meeting that Eragon remembers what he learned when he was with the elves, how a person can change their true name by changing their nature (*Brisingr* p. 320). Although Murtagh admits there is the possibility that this could free Thorn and himself from Galbatorix, he tells Eragon that Galbatorix has been creating name-slaves for more than a hundred years and that he must have anticipated that loophole. In fact, he even believes that the king probably has a spell in place that will alert him if a person attempts to change their nature and force that person to return to his palace, so that he can reinforce the bindings (*Brisingr* p. 321).

The idea that he might gain freedom, even for a moment, only to lose it again is just too painful for him to consider, and so he refuses to even attempt to make a change. Anyway, he says, what sort of change should he undergo? Because he considers himself a good person, the only change he can see undergoing would have him becoming more like Galbatorix (*Brisingr* pp. 319–321)! So what can he do to change his name in order to escape Galbatorix's control? The first thing that he will have to do is to truly know himself, so that he can learn his own name. For if you don't know your own nature, you'll never know your own name, and there's no way you can change who you are.

In *Brisingr*, when Eragon asks Oromis to tell him his true name, Oromis replies that even though he probably could, he won't:

> *"If your desire is to better understand yourself, Eragon, then seek to discover your true name on your own....A person must earn enlightenment, Eragon. It is not handed down to you by others, regardless of how revered they be."* (*Brisingr* p. 642)

As Eragon had suggested to Murtagh that he change his nature in order to change his name before he had this conversation with Oromis, he probably didn't fully understand what he was asking Murtagh to attempt. In fact, I'm not certain whether he completely understood what Oromis's reply meant, as he didn't react at all to what he said. He was still thinking of someone's true name only in terms of how it could be used magically, not what it could mean to a person in terms of understanding himself or herself. He probably still doesn't quite understand the implications of what it means to change one's nature.

There will come a time when Eragon is going to have to go through the process of learning his own name, though, if he hopes to survive the upcoming final confrontation with Galbatorix. Arya has told him that knowledge of the king's true name is not only useless information but potentially fatal, as Galbatorix has cast a spell that will kill anybody trying to use his true name in a spell (*Brisingr* p. 208). Unfortunately, the king has the ability and the desire to use names as a weapon. He has made it clear that, if given the opportunity, he has every intention of controlling Eragon and Saphira by those means. Eragon has to realize that there is a good chance that he could suffer the torment that Murtagh is undergoing unless he's able to devise a means of protecting himself. The only way he can do that is by learning his true name through understanding his own nature. Once he knows himself that well, he could, if he wanted to, change aspects of his character sufficiently to change his name.

What's in a Name?

If you don't think the threat is real, remember back to the beginning of *Brisingr* when the Ra'zac tries to bargain with Eragon and offers up the following information: "He [Galbatorix] has almossst found the *name*" (*Brisingr* p. 65). He then refuses to say any more except, "The *name*! The true *name*!" (*Brisingr* p. 65). What other name, true name, aside from Eragon's, would Galbatorix be desperately searching for? When Eragon presses the creature for more information, it responds that it can't tell him any more—not that it won't—so you have to wonder whether the Ra'zac and their parents were name-slaves, like others whom the king controlled. It would make sense, considering that nobody could figure out how the king was able to convince such evil creatures to do his bidding (*Brisingr* p. 65).

So what's in a name, and will a true name play a significant role in the final outcome of the battle for Alagaësia? We know that Eragon and the Varden won't be able to use Galbatorix's name against him, even if they were to discover it, because of the spell he has cast to protect himself from anybody using it against him. However, that doesn't mean that a true name won't play a significant role in deciding the final outcome of the war. For if Galbatorix manages to find out Eragon's true name and control him in the same manner that he controls Murtagh, can you see any hope that he will be overthrown?

However, if Murtagh were somehow able to change his nature enough to change his true name and then join Eragon and the Varden in the fight against Galbatorix, their chances of defeating the king would increase tremendously. With two Dragon Riders fighting for the resistance, one could concentrate on leading the armies into battle. The other could either take part in trying to rescue the third egg, search for Galbatorix's stash of hearts of hearts in order to weaken his source of magic, or do whatever else might be necessary to find a magical means of overcoming the king.

Finding out your true name is a voyage of self-discovery that won't increase your magical powers or make it harder for an opponent to beat you in a battle of arms. Yet, in spite of that, it is of vital importance that Eragon discover his true nature and his name before Galbatorix does. For then he can take steps to change it and prevent the king from being able to make him a name-slave. In the time we've known Eragon, it's obvious that he has undergone significant changes, but how many of them have really made any difference to his true nature? Has he really changed that much from the impatient, impetuous, and hot-headed farm boy whom we met way back when in *Eragon*?

Although he has a vague idea of what it takes to discover a true name from his experiences with Sloan, is he capable of being honest enough with himself to look in the mirror and see himself for who he truly is? He'd better be, because I predict that the fate of Alagaësia will depend on it.

Chapter 10

Eldunarí: Heart of Hearts

The topic of Eldunarí—a dragon's heart of hearts—has been broached in earlier chapters. It is one of the possible explanations for Galbatorix's extraordinary power, and it could figure into resolving the battle for Alagaësia. Although I offered a brief description of an Eldunarí earlier, it's only appropriate that we turn to the source for a more detailed definition—straight from the "dragon's mouth":

> *"Unlike with most creatures," he [Glaedr] said, "a dragon's consciousness does not reside solely within our skulls. There is in our chests a hard, gemlike object, similar in composition to our scales, called the Eldunarí, which means 'the heart of hearts.'… [I]f we wish, we can transfer our consciousness into the Eldunarí. Then it will acquire the same color as our scales and begin to glow like a coal. If a dragon*

> *has done this, the Eldunarí will outlast the decay*
> *of their flesh, and a dragon's essence may live on*
> *indefinitely."* (*Brisingr* p. 628)

If you're having a hard time grasping the magnitude of what Glaedr is saying, try thinking about it in terms of yourself. Imagine that somehow there were a way that you could transfer your ability to think and express emotions into a vessel that would ensure those capabilities lived on after your body had given out. You would be in a state that was the opposite of a coma, where your body continues to function but your thinking and your emotional self has, for all intents and purposes, shut down. You'd continue to exist as an entity with the ability to think and feel, but without the capacity to experience that which requires a body. Seeing, hearing, tasting, touching, and smelling would all be things of the past. As far as the physical world goes, you would have to rely on the memory of things you had experienced in order to give it definition or trust those around you to describe it to you.

So why would any creature even consider doing something like this? It doesn't seem like much of an existence, does it? Well, as Glaedr explains to Eragon, and as we've come to understand throughout the series, dragons, especially those who have chosen Riders, are more than a little different from the rest of us. Although for many dragons the idea of living without being able to sense or experience the world around them, except as impressions of it were relayed to them through the mind of another, wasn't appealing, even in the days before Dragon Riders there were dragons who transferred their consciousness into their Eldunarí. Sometimes it was by accident;

if death came on them suddenly — in battle, for instance — they could have panicked while dying and fled from the sensations of death into the shelter of their Eldunarí. However, there were also dragons who had lived so long that they no longer cared about the physical world and decided to devote themselves to the search for enlightenment by abandoning the distractions of the physical world (*Brisingr* p. 633).

(If you are at all familiar with any of the Eastern religions — Hinduism or Buddhism, for instance — you have probably heard of humans who have spent their lives in a similar manner. The usual purpose for doing this is for the person to gain a deeper understanding of the nature of life and existence, in order to help them live a life that is as close as possible to the ideal state, nirvana. Religions, such as Hinduism, that believe in reincarnation see the achievement of nirvana as the ultimate goal. Once it's attained, you are freed from returning to earth as a physical being ever again and become one with the universe. Supposedly, it takes a human many lifetimes to reach the state of purity required to achieve nirvana, and only those willing to surrender all physical attachments are able to do so. As yet another example of their superiority to humans, dragons appear to be able to accomplish this feat at will.)

Even before the days of the Dragon Riders, therefore, there were those dragons who transferred their essences into the Eldunarí, but in the days of the Riders it became far more common an occurrence. In fact, according to Oromis and Glaedr, by the later stages of the partnership between Riders and dragons, many dragons not only transferred themselves over to their Eldunarí, but carried out the more dangerous second phase of the process: surrendering their heart of hearts to another being. For a dragon did not have to wait until he or she was dying to carry out the transition. The dragon could do it while still alive and give it over for safekeeping to anyone of their choosing. Any Rider who possessed his or her dragon's Eldunarí would not only be able to communicate with their dragon, without regard to distance, they would also be able to draw upon their dragon's strength through it in order to bolster their spells (*Brisingr* p. 630). You can see why a dragon might share their heart of hearts with their Rider. Think of the advantages a Rider who possessed a dragon's heart of hearts would have over Riders who didn't. Unfortunately, it was this habit of sharing hearts that allowed Galbatorix to gain his incredible magical strength and gave him the opportunity to destroy the other Riders and conquer the kingdom.

By killing Riders who traveled with their dragon's Eldunarí, he was able to enslave the dragon's consciousness and utilize its magical power, in spite of the fact that when a dragon's Rider is killed, the dragon will usually die as well. Even if their physical body died, they weren't able to escape his clutches if their Eldunarí fell into the king's hands. Although it may have taken him some time to enslave that first Eldunarí, once he began to accumulate them, his power began to grow exponentially. Each subsequent enslavement would have become easier, until he was finally strong enough to overthrow the Dragon Riders and establish himself as king (*Brisingr* p. 631).

Before the days of the Dragon Riders, wild dragons had their own repository for the Eldunarí of those dragons who had transferred their essences into them and whose bodies had died. After the alliance between Riders and dragons was forged, all of the Eldunarí already in existence, and any new Eldunarí not given to an individual Rider, were stored in the Riders' capital city of Doru Araeba. So not only does Galbatorix have the Eldunarí of those Riders whom he killed, he also has in his possession nearly all of the Eldunarí ever created. It's hard to imagine just how powerful he must be, with all that wisdom and magical energy to draw upon. It's no wonder that he's virtually unstoppable (*Brisingr* p. 636)!

The king's access to the Eldunarí of many dragons also helps to explain how Murtagh became such a powerful magician so quickly. Both times that Eragon has met Murtagh in battle, he's noticed that he could hear what sounded like a confused chorus of voices underneath Murtagh's own thoughts. During their second battle, he wondered if Murtagh were being assisted by a group of magicians, much as he was being aided by Arya and the twelve elven spellcasters, who acted as his bodyguard and loaned him their power when he was casting spells (*Brisingr* pp. 316–329). However, once he learns of the existence of Eldunarí, he understands that what he was hearing were actually the "voices" of the various dragons who had been enslaved by Galbatorix to fight for him. Murtagh has become so powerful with them in his possession that, even with the assistance offered by Arya and the others, Eragon is still only barely able to fend him off. Their second battle ends in a draw.

However, Murtagh and Galbatorix don't control all of the Eldunarí, and — as a final gesture of hope and blessing — Glaedr gives Eragon his heart of hearts just before he and Oromis head off to what ends up being their final battle (*Brisingr* pp. 694–695). Now, it's no small gift for any Rider to receive the Eldunarí of another Rider's dragon, and at the time Glaedr gives Eragon his, he is the oldest living dragon in Alagaësia, which means that his gift is especially powerful. Of course, if all goes according to plan, Eragon will be taking up the mantle of teacher to the next generation of Dragon Riders and will need to draw upon the wisdom and knowledge that's been accumulated over the years by Glaedr in order to train them. However, Glaedr also knows that if Eragon is to have any hope of defeating Galbatorix, he's going to need either Oromis's and his assistance from a distance or else (should Glaedr die in battle) Glaedr's energy and his accumulated wisdom.

Yet will even that be enough for Eragon to defeat Galbatorix? We see at the end of *Brisingr* how easily the king defeats Oromis and Glaedr (pp. 732–735), which means that Eragon must find a way to counter the power the king has amassed from his years of enslaving the Eldunarí of Alagaësia's dragons. Somehow, Eragon must find where these hearts of hearts are stored and break Galbatorix's control over them. The problem is that he doesn't know where they are stored. And even if he were to find out where they were, he would have to get by any wards or other protections that have been set around them. You can bet that if the king has made it suicide to try to rescue the last dragon egg, his stash of Eldunarí are going to be pretty well guarded.

At some point in Book Four, Eragon will be forced to deal with the problem of the Eldunarí. In order to do so, he will first have to discover their whereabouts and then somehow manage to elude the protections that Galbatorix has set up around them. However, even if he somehow manages to do that, how would he go about freeing the dragons from the king's control? Will he end up having to destroy all of them, sending the ancient dragons of Alagaësia to their deaths, in order to free them? As long as the king has control of the hundreds of Eldunarí that he is suspected of having enslaved, there isn't a spell that Eragon can cast that the king wouldn't be able to overcome or overpower.

Although that might sound horrible, think of it from the dragon's point of view. As Glaedr says in *Brisingr* when he is describing what an Eldunarí is, most dragons don't like the idea of trapping their consciousness in a heart of hearts: "To be unable to move of your own volition...would be a difficult existence to embrace for most any creature, but especially dragons, who are the freest of all beings" (*Brisingr* p. 633). Now, imagine how they must feel if they not only can't move but are being forced to carry out the despicable ideas of Galbatorix. There's a good chance that, unlike Murtagh, who would rather live and carry out the evil of the king, these enslaved dragons would prefer death to their current state.

It seems that Christopher Paolini has set Eragon a nearly impossible task: he must deal with the Eldunarí that are in Galbatorix's possession in order to overcome the king. But the author has given Eragon a couple of avenues through which he might be able to at least find where the hearts of hearts have been stored. I still say it is no coincidence that Angela's herb shop, which Eragon wanders into, is located next door to the house of Jeod, Brom's old friend from the Varden (*Eragon*

p. 198). Not only does Jeod go on to play an important role in helping Roran and the rest of the villagers from Carvahall escape from Teirm, but he is the one who, earlier, discovered the existence of the secret passage into Galbatorix's castle, which allowed the Varden to steal Saphira's egg. Angela may not be a member of the Varden, but she is as key a member of the resistance against the Empire as anyone, so it can't have been an accident that Paolini has them living beside each other.

So what does that have to do with the Eldunarí? Well, first of all, think back to that first meeting between Eragon and Angela and the two pieces of advice that Solembum the werecat give to Eragon. The first one, "When the time comes and you need a weapon, look under the roots of the Menoa tree" (*Eragon* p. 206), has already paid off by providing the star metal needed to make Eragon's new sword, Brisingr. The second piece of advice, "when all seems lost and your power is insufficient, go to the Rock of Kuthian and speak your name to open the Vault of Souls" (*Eragon* p. 206), remains as mysterious and unsolved as it did on the day it was uttered.

Part of the problem is that, up to this point, nobody that Eragon has asked has any idea what or where the Rock of Kuthian is. Although Oromis said that the name sounded familiar, he couldn't place it (*Brisingr* p. 639). But perhaps Eragon hasn't asked the right person yet. Remember that when we first meet Jeod that Brom, who hasn't seen his old friend in twenty years, is surprised that he's become a merchant and not remained a scholar. Of all the people Eragon knows, Jeod probably knows more about the history of Alagaësia than anybody, including the elves. Although the elves had built the hidden passage into Galbatorix's castle, it was Jeod who found out about the hidden passage by studying old texts (*Eragon* p. 185).

Now, fast forward to *Brisingr*, when Eragon visits Jeod and his wife, Helen, at their tent in the Varden encampment. When Eragon asks him what he is doing for the Varden, Jeod tells him that they have him searching through old texts, looking for any reference he can find to other passageways into the king's castle in the hope that they can recover the final dragon's egg. At the same time, Jeod gives Eragon a present, a copy of *Domia abr Wyrda* (*Dominance of Fate*), the complete history of Alagaësia, which had been banned by Galbatorix (*Brisingr* p. 288). The book not only tells the history of mortal humanity, it stretches back to the days of the Grey Folk, the creators of magic and the ancient language. If the whereabouts of the Vault of Souls and the Rock of Kuthian is going to be found, it seems only logical that a good place to start would be to read *Dominance of Fate* — or consult a scholar who has read it.

As to what the Vault of Souls and the Rock of Kuthian have to do with Eldunarí, well, I would think the connection would be obvious. A heart of hearts is, for all intents and purposes, the equivalent of a soul. What else do you know of that contains all the awareness of a being and continues to live on after the physical body has reached the end of its days? Remember, Solembum tells Eragon the name of the place in the common tongue, not the ancient language, so we don't know its true name or its purpose. For all we know, it might be a repository of Eldunarí that predates the alliance between the elves and the dragons and has long been forgotten. Of course, it might be something else altogether, but we won't know until Eragon is able to find and open it.

Of course, there still remains the problem of how Eragon is going to find the time to accomplish all of these tasks while carrying on the war with Galbatorix. Whether it's discovering the whereabouts of Galbatorix's stash of Eldunarí and wresting control of it away from the king — either by destroying the hearts of hearts or casting a spell that breaks his connection to them — or whether it's finding the mysterious Vault of Souls and gaining admission to it, it appears that he and Saphira are going to have to learn how to be two places at once if they are to win the war.

Because knowing the king's true name is of no use in fighting him, the Eldunarí are the only means that Paolini has provided Eragon with for defeating Galbatorix. No matter how powerful that possessing Glaedr's heart of hearts makes him, it won't be sufficient to defeat Galbatorix. Although as long as he's able to prevent the king from learning that he has it, there's a chance he can use it to either defeat or rescue Thorn and Murtagh the next time they meet in battle. This just might give him the edge he's been lacking up until now. The best-case scenario would see him somehow using the extra power of the Eldunarí to release the other pair from the king's power. Perhaps Glaedr will be able to figure out Murtagh's true name and a way for him to change his nature sufficiently that his name changes enough for him to be freed. Even if he's only able to put them out of action temporarily by injuring them enough that they can't fight, it might buy him enough time so that he can set out on the quest for either the Vault of Souls or the king's repository of Eldunarí.

No matter what else happens in the events to come, unless the riddle of the Eldunarí is solved, there is no way for Eragon and the Varden to win. So Eragon had better hope that he can find the answer soon. Otherwise, all will have been for naught and all of his friends will die.

Chapter 11

Matters of the Heart

Although the question of romance for the characters in the Inheritance cycle hasn't featured quite as prominently as it would normally in the lives of young people, there are still some romantic entanglements that will have to be unraveled before the series comes to its conclusion. Leaving Eragon aside for the moment—although his affairs of the heart will be our primary concern, of course—we'll start by focusing on some of the secondary relationships and their potential for success or failure.

Jeod and Helen

The relationship that has looked to be the one least likely to endure from the moment we met the couple has been that of Jeod and his wife, Helen. The first thing we learn from Jeod about his marriage to Helen is how much of a disappointment it has been to her. We get a good view of her resentment when Eragon and Brom first meet her when they are staying with them during their sojourn in Teirm. The whole time they are there, she appears to be doing a continuous slow burn over their presence (*Eragon* pp. 181–221).

Yet when she finds out why Jeod's business has been failing for so long — because he has been supplying the Varden, in defiance of the king — Helen is more upset because he hadn't confided in her, rather than because his business is failing. Then, when he gives her the opportunity to leave him and return to her father's house when he agrees to help Roran seize a ship to help him and the villagers of Carvahall continue their flight to the relative safety of the Varden, she comes with them (*Eldest* p. 511). In spite of the dangers, in spite of the uncertain future, and in spite of the past disappointments, she'd still rather be with him than return to her father's house. Perhaps there's an element of pride in her decision — she doesn't want to appear a failure in the eyes of her family — but that's not the whole story. Remember how surprised Roran is when she shows up on the gangplank of the ship as they are getting ready to set sail for Surda in *Eldest*? And remember that he thinks to himself, after Helen has stowed her belongings below deck and come to stand next to Jeod, that he's "never seen a happier man" (*Eldest* p. 511)? In spite of all their arguments, and in spite of her resentment over the way things have turned out for her, Helen not only remains true to her husband at this dangerous time, but her presence alone is able to bring

Jeod great happiness. If she didn't have any feelings for him, do you really think that would be possible?

However, this moment of rapprochement seems to be only short-lived. Perhaps the period of peace was inspired by Jeod's status as a man of action. Helen has never seen this side of him before. All of a sudden, he is a dashing hero, risking life and limb against huge odds to help those in peril. But when Eragon first visits the couple among the Varden in *Brisingr* (p. 279), it's only to find that Helen is again feeling resentful about her status. Instead of having servants to wait on her, as she is used to, she is forced cook and clean for herself. Somehow she had come to believe that because Jeod had performed such an important service for the Varden—discovering the means to steal the egg that hatched Saphira—he would have been rewarded with a high rank and the living circumstances to go with it. Instead, she finds herself living in a tent like a common soldier.

Her attitude undergoes a massive transformation when she is given the chance to do something more than housework. Although it may seem rather shallow and cold for her happiness to depend so much on the material things and status that the lump of gold that Eragon offers her represents (*Brisingr* p. 290), perhaps one needs to look at her attitude from another perspective. Remember that she is much younger than Jeod, and for most of their marriage she has had nothing to do but run the household, look pretty, and watch as her husband has seemingly allowed their lives to be ruined. Not only had he not trusted her with the knowledge of what he was really doing, she was left with nothing to do. She wasn't anything close to being an equal partner in their relationship. Helen was, for all intents and purposes, a trophy wife.

Helen is a proud and intelligent woman, and even in the best of times that sort of life must have been incredibly dissatisfying. Remember what she says to Eragon when he gives her the gold? She tells him that she comes from a family of traders and merchants. She will, she says, parlay his gift into the beginnings of a fortune. Is it any wonder she's been so unhappy with her marriage? How frustrating it must have been for her to have to concern herself solely with running a household all day long. Think of the other strong female characters in this book, Arya and Nasuada, for instance. Can you imagine either of them confining their energies solely to husband and household?

Like them, Helen needs to be out in the world in order to be happy, and now that she is, she will not only feel better about herself, but it can only improve her relationship with Jeod. As long as Jeod learns his lesson and doesn't hide information from her again in the future — if he treats her as a real, active partner in their relationship — there's no reason that their marriage will not only last but thrive.

The importance of their happiness as a couple shouldn't be underestimated either, as Jeod is likely to play a key role in both the future of Alagaësia and in Book Four. With his knowledge of history and lore, he is far more likely to uncover secrets, such as the location of the Vault of Souls, than anyone else is. How much easier will it be for him to accomplish these tasks if his wife is content with her lot? Now that he no longer has to worry about keeping her happy, or whether their marriage will survive, he can devote himself completely to the task at hand.

There was also always the potential for Helen to betray Jeod and the Varden when she was unhappy. Resentment and bitterness can drive people to do things that they wouldn't do under normal circumstances, and who knows what she could have done if her life had continued on in the same way? All that has changed, because it's thanks to the Varden—and Eragon specifically—that she has the opportunity to do something with her life that she finds meaningful. Their future may not be any more certain than that of anybody fighting against the Empire, but at least Helen now has some semblance of control over what she does and can chart her own course, rather than being dependent on Jeod.

Jeod and Helen are the only mature couple to play a significant role in the series. And their relationship is also important for what it has to offer Eragon in terms of teaching him about reality. Remember how he is horrified by the fact that Arya is going to risk her life fighting the Urgals when the Varden are attacked in *Eragon*? Remember her reaction when he is stupid enough to say it's too dangerous (*Eragon* p. 477)? She rips a strip off him. Although he knows better than to do that again, and has come to respect her abilities and powers, he still has a way to go before he understands what it means to be in a relationship of equals.

Jeod and Helen are a prime example of what happens to a couple in an unequal relationship, where one has plenty to do and the other feels stifled. If Eragon has any brains, he will look at their example carefully and consider what he wants from a relationship with Arya — or any woman, for that matter — in that light. However, it's doubtful that he's even thought about their relationship beyond the fact that he's besotted with her. Most likely, he hasn't given any thought to the reality of what it would be like married to a person as independent as she is.

Christopher Paolini is too good an author to include information in his story without a reason, and although Helen and Jeod's relationship might not be central to the series, it serves as a reminder for anybody who cares to see that sometimes love is not enough for a relationship to work. With Eragon's help, they appear to have solved the difficulties in their marriage. But will Eragon be able to apply what he has learned from them to his own love life?

Roran and Katrina

On the surface, this is a match that the gods and goddesses have blessed. For in spite of the odds, Roran and Katrina have not only been reunited but, by the time *Brisingr* comes around, they are safely wed and Katrina is pregnant with their first child (*Brisingr* p. 341). Although they're not leading the life that Roran had envisioned — living happily on a farm with their family — all things considered, they're not doing too badly. Sure, there's always the worry that Roran could be killed fighting Galbatorix, but he's proven himself such an able fighter that even warriors with magical augmentation have a hard time standing up to him in battle. The real concern for Roran's safety would have to be if the king were to take a personal interest in him again because he's Eragon's cousin, or because he's become so important to the Varden's war effort.

Yet in spite of Roran's obvious devotion to Katrina, and her love for him, there has been an underlying disquiet about their relationship from the outset, because her father, Sloan, refused to give her permission to marry. According to the code of their society, if a father refuses a daughter permission to marry and she defies his position, he is within his rights to deny her a dowry (a dowry is the possessions that a woman takes into marriage, and can range from livestock to money) and disinherit her as well. In spite of Sloan's refusal to give his permission for Roran to court Katrina, that young man had proposed to her and she had accepted. For a while, they kept their intentions secret. Sloan was so irate when he found out, he betrayed his fellow villagers to Galbatorix's soldiers, which resulted in both Katrina and himself being captured by the Ra'zac (*Eldest* pp. 194–199).

Yet in spite of her father's irrational behavior, Katrina can't help but still care about what happens to him. For when Eragon and Roran rescue her from the Ra'zac, one of the first things she asks about is her father in the hope that he can be rescued, too (*Brisingr* pp. 54–63). What she doesn't consider is the fact that if Sloan were to return with her, he would be executed for his betrayal of the village and the death of one of the villagers. In order to protect Roran and Katrina's relationship, Eragon lies, telling them that Sloan is dead. Eragon then devises the means to keep Sloan apart from the couple forever. He fears, and rightly so, that the issue of Sloan could cause a division between the two of them that might never heal.

In spite of their happiness, and their love for each other, if Roran were to find out that Sloan was alive, he could be pushed by anger and the need for vengeance to kill him. What do you think that would do to Katrina if her husband killed her father? Although he had disowned her and betrayed her, she still worried about her father. What do you think Katrina would do if she found out that Sloan was still alive and living among the elves? Wouldn't she want to go and make sure that he was all right? Perhaps she might even insist on going and taking care of him if she found out that he was blind and helpless. How do you think Roran would react to that? What would the rest of the villagers think if they found out that Sloan was still alive? Don't you think that they would want him to pay for his crimes?

Sloan still has a role to play in the story, and I fear that it's not a pleasant one. Maybe Roran will find out that Sloan is alive and keep that knowledge from Katrina, only to have her find out that he knew and didn't tell her. This could create serious problems in their relationship—or end it. It's a difficult thing for a daughter to have to choose between her husband and her father, and although Katrina initially chose to be with Roran, that was when they were all still living in the same village and there was always the chance of them reconciling. Now that there is no chance of that happening, if she were forced to choose between them, she might grow to resent Roran because she rejected her father. She could eventually leave Roran over this issue. Or perhaps she would choose her father over him in the first place.

There's one other potential threat to their relationship, of course, and that's Galbatorix. He already knows that Roran will go to any lengths to rescue her, so he's aware that Katrina would be a key to controlling him. Of course, the king could just kill him outright. But Galbatorix is much more devious than that; he would probably rather have Roran either suffer or be in his control, rather than dead. What better way to hurt Roran than to kill Katrina? Or what easier way to control him than by capturing her again and holding her hostage? What's to stop Murtagh and Thorn from doing a quick hit and run of the Varden's camp one night and stealing off with Katrina? Now that she's pregnant, there's probably nothing on earth that would stop Roran from setting out immediately to rescue her, unless he's in jail or tied up.

Although Katrina and Roran are very much in love, there are too many ways in which their relationship can end badly for it to be considered secure. The chances of it surviving the series, although still good, aren't what anybody should consider a sure bet. It would be cruel for Roran to have gone through so much in order to rescue her, only to have her taken away from him in the end, but sometimes life isn't fair.

Saphira

If you ever thought that *you* had troubles when it came to matters of the heart, give a thought to Saphira. When she was born, as far as she knew there existed only one other dragon of the Dragon Riders besides herself: Shruikan, a dragon of the Forsworn. Shruikan had been enslaved by Galbatorix and driven mad in the process. Two unhatched dragon eggs, representing her potential mates, also existed. So her only real hope, she assumed, rested in one of the other eggs hatching a male with whom she might have a chance of perpetuating the species. Of course, when she met Glaedr, she became immediately infatuated — see her behavior in *Eldest*. It took a while for Saphira to settle down and accept the fact that he was only ever going to be her teacher and stop flirting with him. The truth of the matter for Saphira is that love might not have much to do with her choice of mate, for if she wants her species to survive, she's going to have to mate with one of the two, or maybe even both of the dragons who hatch out of the eggs that Galbatorix holds.

The real problem is, of course, the fact that both of her potential mates are in Galbatorix's control. And unless she were enslaved, she's certainly not going to produce more dragon eggs for the king to control. Now, we know that one of them has hatched as the male dragon Thorn, who is joined with Murtagh, and although the other is a male, its future still remains a mystery. Of course, whether Saphira mates with either of them will depend on whether she and Eragon are able to defeat the Empire, and on whether both Thorn and the other dragon survive the battle. Because we don't know when the third and final dragon is going to hatch, and have only Galbatorix's word for it that it will be a male, the only potential mate in existence for her at present is Thorn.

Saphira and Thorn are on opposite sides in the war, and she may have to kill him in order to even have a chance of fighting Galbatorix. The other major stumbling block in the way of the two of them becoming an item is whether Thorn has suffered any permanent damage from the enforced growth he has undergone at the hands of Galbatorix. At the beginning of *Brisingr*, when Saphira and Eragon meet Thorn and Murtagh in battle for the second time (*Brisingr* pp. 312–329), they are amazed that he has grown so much in such a short period of time. He is described as being "barely older than a hatchling, but he was already nearly as large as Saphira" (*Brisingr* p. 317). During the lull in their fight, when Eragon is trying to convince his half-brother that he and Thorn can escape from the king's enslavement, both he and Saphira feel a great pity for the dragon. He's so obviously sad and confused about why he'd been brought into the world "merely so Galbatorix could enslave him, abuse him, and force him to destroy other beings' lives" (*Brisingr* p. 319).

Remember, when Galbatorix's own dragon was killed and he killed another Rider and enslaved his dragon, Shruikan, the poor creature was driven insane from the torment. The longer that Thorn remains under the king's control, forced to do things that go against his nature and his will, the greater the likelihood of him suffering permanent mental and emotional damage, which could prevent him from ever having a normal relationship with another dragon. If Saphira and Eragon are able to finish off the battle quickly enough, there's a good chance that he might yet still have time for his emotional and mental development to catch up to his physical maturity, giving him a good chance to lead a normal life. So, as if they didn't have incentive enough to finish this war quickly, not only does any chance of Saphira mating ride on the speed with which they bring it to a conclusion, the very future of dragons depends on it.

For Saphira, the issue isn't one of romance; it's a matter of ensuring the survival of her species. Galbatorix covets her because he'd like to force her to breed with both his dragon and with Thorn, thus ensuring his supply of eggs and control of any future Riders. Although there would be no question of her being forced to do anything against her will in the event of the Varden winning, she may decide of her own free will to breed for the sake of preserving her species and ensuring the future of the Dragon Riders. It doesn't look as though Saphira is destined to have any romance in her life, which means that when it comes to companionship, she'll just have to make do with her link to Eragon and possibly her (potential) offspring.

Eragon

Of course, the primary concern when it comes to love interests is what's going to happen with Eragon. More specifically, Eragon has had a crush on Arya from the moment she first appeared in his dreams, when she was held captive by Durza. Eragon was only sixteen when he first met her. He had little experience with women and was captivated by the exotic and beautiful elf. However, not only has she not reciprocated his feelings, she's told him in no uncertain terms that a relationship between the two of them would be impossible. Aside from the age difference, which she cited as the major stumbling block (*Eldest* pp. 473–474), there are vast cultural differences between the two of them.

Part of that is due to the different perspectives on life that the two races have. Unlike humans, elves are immortal. That is to say, they don't die of old age. They can, however, be killed. This means, for example, the concept of "working for a living" is completely alien to them, as they don't share humanity's need to accumulate wealth or material possessions within a fixed time. They are able to supply themselves with the necessities of life without any of the toil that we mortals normally have to experience in order to survive. Despite the fact that Eragon's life span has been extended because he is a Dragon Rider, what matters is that he's been conditioned to think and act like a mortal and can no more understand the thought patterns or emotions of an elf than we can understand those of a frog or an angel.

Of course, there's also the fact that elves view relationships very differently than humans do. According to what Arya told Eragon, it's rare for elves to marry, and the concept of "'Til death do us part" would be completely unheard of. They are realistic enough to realize that when you're immortal, the chances of wanting to stay with the same partner forever are slim. One need only think about the difficulties most mortals in our world have in sustaining a marriage, and you'll have to admit they have a pretty valid point. Now, there's nothing saying that Eragon and Arya have to marry in order to have a successful relationship, but there are other stumbling blocks to a happy relationship between them.

Eragon has been close to obsessive when it comes to Arya, and he feels as though his happiness depends upon how she feels about him. Even when Arya tells him that if he continues to press her on the matter, she will sever all ties with him, he refuses to stop his pursuit (*Eldest* p. 474). At the end of *Eldest*, it certainly looks as if there's no chance of a relationship between the two of them. However, when Arya meets up with

Eragon near the beginning of *Brisingr*, when he is returning to the Varden after killing the Ra'zac, she seems to have softened her stance somewhat. She's at least the most open she's been with him up to that point, telling him about the elf whom she had cared for deeply and how he had been killed by Durza's Urgals. Of course, Eragon shows how he is still far from being as emotionally mature as her when he feels jealous of her dead friend (*Brisingr* p. 197).

Still, there are other signs that Arya is warming toward him. Just before Eragon and Saphira fly into battle against Murtagh and Thorn in *Brisingr*, she starts to say something, but stumbles and stops. Maybe she wants to say something personal, such as "Take care" or "Stay safe," but backs off (*Brisingr* p. 316). Then, once the battle is under way, she's back to business as usual. This brings us to the nub of the problem in their relationship. Arya has devoted herself to the cause of the Varden and ensuring the safety of their dragon egg for longer than Eragon has been alive. She's paid a steep price for her choice; she's been as good as exiled from her home and she's been estranged from her mother. As far as she's concerned, Eragon is, first and foremost, the Dragon Rider upon whom everybody's hopes rest. Arya has worked too hard and too long to see it all ruined because Eragon can't control his emotions.

Eragon, on the other hand, has put her on a pedestal as his ideal romantic figure and has a hard time staying focused on what he should be doing when she's around. In fact, he is so immature and besotted with her that he doesn't stop to think how his behavior will affect her. In other words, he is a typical selfish adolescent human with a severe case of hormones.

Even though he's finally learned not to say anything to her about how he feels, it doesn't stop him from hoping that somehow something will change in her attitude toward him.

The chances of Eragon and Arya becoming a couple are still pretty slim. Remember that the prophecy didn't say that the love he felt for the noble person would ever be reciprocated. As things stand at the end of *Brisingr*, they may end up being good companions and close friends, but that's about it. However, that doesn't mean that there won't be love in Eragon's life before the series ends, for there is another person who fits the description of the person in the prophecy. That person is Nasuada, the leader of the Varden. Now, unlike Arya, she is not the daughter of a queen. But she is of a noble family and she is a leader of her people, the nomads of Alagaësia. Although Eragon has never thought about her in a romantic way, and she's never expressed anything either way about him, there have been moments when we have seen the potential for them to have a relationship.

After Eragon's initial battle with Murtagh, nobody knew whether he was alive, captured, or dead. When he returned to Nasuada's tent to report in, she ran to him and threw her arms around him — not exactly typical behavior for a leader of an army when it comes to one of her captains, no matter how important he is to their cause (*Eldest* p. 660). True, Eragon and Saphira are vital to the Varden's war effort, but that doesn't explain the enthusiasm of her greeting, especially when it's compared with Arya's reaction at the same time.

Then there's the time when Eragon has just returned from killing the Ra'zac, and he and Nasuada are walking about the camp, arm in arm. They are on the way to a surprise welcome home party she's organized for him, and he's amazed at how comfortable he feels talking to her and the feelings being with her engender in him (*Brisingr* p. 245). Without knowing how it's happened, a bond has formed between the two of them that is much different from soldier and commander. His lack of experience with women means that he doesn't realize that what he feels for her is far more real than the romantic notions he has about Arya.

This book has already outlined how they could overcome the stumbling block of his immortality if the final dragon egg were to hatch for her after the war was over, giving them the same life expectancy. It would also give Nasuada a reason to give up her leadership role and leave Alagaësia to join Eragon in his life among the elves, where he could begin her instruction as a Dragon Rider. Sure, quite a few conditions would have to be met in order for them to be together, but it still seems as likely — if not more likely — as Eragon and Arya ever getting together. The other thing to remember is that Nasuada is a major character in the story in her own right. We spend quite a bit of time with her and see the world through her eyes when Eragon isn't around, which isn't the case with Arya. There has to be a reason for that, other than to show us what's going on with the Varden. I believe that we've grown to know Nasuada this well in order to prepare the way for her and Eragon to discover, by the end of the series, that they are in love.

Love and romance are tricky things to predict, as the heart can be as fickle as the wind, which blows one way this moment and another way the next. In terms of the characters in the

Inheritance cycle, everything really depends on the outcome of the war they are fighting against Galbatorix. Any predictions made here, of course, depend on the eventual defeat of the king, for until that's assured, nothing much else can be guaranteed. That said, look for no major changes in our two existing couples, Jeod and Helen and Roran and Katrina, although the latter two have the specter of Sloan hanging over them. Saphira seems destined to have no romance in her life. However, that doesn't mean that she won't find love. She may create the equally powerful bond that exists between mother and child. Eragon will recover from his infatuation with Arya and discover a deeper and truer love for Nasuada. However, even in times of peace, Cupid's arrows take their own path, heedless of the wishes of mortals and immortals alike. Who among us can truly predict where they will land?

Chapter 12

Elva: Power and Responsibility

Throughout the course of the first three books of the Inheritance cycle, Christopher Paolini has reiterated that personal power must be balanced by personal responsibility. Whether in Eragon's training as a Dragon Rider—when Oromis refuses to teach him certain forms of magic because he fears that he is not ready to deal with them—or in the reactions of other characters to Eragon's abilities, the subject keeps coming up. It's only natural, of course. The Varden and the people of the Empire have been dealing for years with a king who has exercised absolute power for his own gain.

To most people, Saphira and Eragon represent almost unlimited power, and they can't help but see the potential for one autocrat to be replaced by another. Even Eragon's closest allies, although they hide it well most of the time, are subject to those fears. Here is how King Orrin of Surda reacts to Eragon's treatment of Katrina's father, Sloan:

> *"For he who has the audacity to determine who should live and who should die no longer serves the law but dictates the law. And however benevolent you might be, that would be no good thing for our species....Do you understand, Eragon? You are so dangerous, we are forced to acknowledge the danger to your face and hope that you are one of the few people able to resist the lure of power."* (Brisingr pp. 238–239)

Now, obviously nobody believes that Eragon will turn into another Galbatorix, but they are still concerned about how he uses his power. For there are aspects of Eragon's power that not even the wisest of the elves can explain, such as the fact that his sword, Brisingr, bursts into flame whenever Eragon says its name (*Brisingr* p. 682), even though he's not trying to cast the spell to create fire. Together, he and Saphira represent such an unknown quantity in terms of their potential that even Oromis is taken aback on occasion:

> *"In all my years, I have never met anyone such as the two of you....You change the world with your whims."* (Eldest p. 295)

As with anybody new to power of any kind, the real danger that Eragon represents is what he might do out of ignorance or by accident, as he has shown no inclination to use his power to gain power over others. As for those who think that he wants to set himself up as a replacement for Galbatorix, he makes it perfectly clear that he would consider ruling Alagaësia only if nobody else suitable were available to do the job. He would stay on in that role only until somebody suitable could be found to replace him (*Eragon* p. 443).

However, the fact can't be ignored that, outside a handful of people, he's probably the most powerful person in not only the country but the whole continent. On top of that, Eragon has shown he's not above making precipitous decisions, acting out of resentment, or being obstinate to the point of pigheadedness, any of which could accidentally lead him to misuse his power, with possibly disastrous results. As his training has progressed, he has learned to restrain himself, but even in his final lessons with Oromis during *Brisingr*, he still shows signs of his immaturity through his reactions to Saphira withholding her knowledge of the Eldunarí (p. 629).

However, if Eragon ever wants a reminder of the consequences of the accidental misuse of power, he need look no further than the character of Elva — the baby he attempted to bless when he first arrived among the Varden. At the time, especially as Saphira had complemented Eragon's verbal blessing by marking the baby with the sign of the Riders — the gedwëy ignasia — on her forehead, everybody thought what he had done was wonderful. Those among the Varden who had infants were eager for Eragon and Saphira to repeat what they had done with their own children (*Eragon* pp. 428–429). It wasn't until Elva discovered the true nature of her "gift" that the damage Eragon had caused was revealed: the wrong form of one word in the ancient language had turned the intended blessing into a curse.

"Atra guliä un ilian tauthr ono un atra ono waíse skölir fra rauthr," he had intoned (*Eragon* p. 428) — thinking that if any words had the power to shield the child from any future tragedy, those would do the trick. Unfortunately, as he found out later when he repeated the phrase to Oromis, instead of casting a spell that would shield the child from harm, he had turned her into someone who is driven to shield others from pain. For instead of using the form of the word for "shielded," *sköliro,* so that the blessing would say, "May luck and happiness follow you and may you be shielded from misfortune," he used *skölir,* the form of the word that meant "shield," so the second part of his blessing was actually, "may you be a shield from misfortune" (*Eldest* pp. 294–295).

Although that might not sound so bad on the surface, when Oromis spells out the difference between the two, we see the truly awful fate to which Eragon has condemned Elva. For instead of protecting her from harm, the spell will ensure that she feels the misery and pain of everybody around her and also be compelled to save them from whatever was causing them to suffer (*Eldest* pp. 294–295).

Eragon is shocked to discover the harm he has done, and vows that he will do anything and everything in his power to counteract the curse. It's not until you meet Elva that you truly understand the transformation that she has undergone. It's through the eyes of Nasuada that we see her for the first time after she received Eragon's blessing, and what she finds appalls her. For instead of an infant, she is confronted with a child who appears to be around three or four, and who is far more articulate than any child of that age has the right to be. Not only has the spell changed her in the way already described, it has also given her the power to change herself physically; she has managed to force herself to age and learn how to talk (*Eldest* pp. 332–333).

During that first meeting between Nasuada and Elva, we get a brief glimpse of what her power allows her to do. Not only is she able to discern exactly what Nasuada's deepest fear is, but she knows just what to say in order to evoke a powerful emotional reaction in her based on it. In this case, she offers Nasuada relief by assuring her that history will judge her a worthy successor to her father for having the bravery to move the Varden into Surda and for taking the battle to Galbatorix, not waiting for him to attack. What Nasuada finds most frightening is how easily Elva is able to induce a reaction in herself. She is struck by her ability to manipulate people's emotions. For now, though, she need not worry, as Elva reassures her that she wants to do anything she can to help end the war, because the longer the war continues, the longer she will suffer. Every time a person is injured, Elva feels it. Every time a person mourns a death, Elva feels it. And she is compelled to try to help the sufferer deal with it. If she doesn't, the pain she experiences reaches a point where she becomes physically sick (*Eldest* pp. 333–334).

Part of what makes Elva so useful to the Varden, as Nasuada discovers, is that she is also able to predict what a person will do about two to three hours prior to them acting. When Galbatorix sends assassins after Nasuada, it's Elva who not only prevents one attempt, but is able to track down the rest of the assassins by their emotions (*Eldest* pp. 519–520).

From that point on, Nasuada and Elva are never parted. Elva lends valuable assistance to Nasuada, helping her to deal with the daily political infighting among her advisers. There's nothing like being able to read a political opponent's mind to keep them in check and circumvent their attempts to chip away at your authority!

Unfortunately, no matter how useful Elva is to the Varden's cause and to Nasuada personally, that doesn't change the fact that she suffers horribly because of what Eragon did. Therefore, upon his return from helping rescue Katrina, he decides that he must at least attempt to rectify the damage he caused by casting a new spell. Hopefully, this new spell will at least mitigate the damage, if not heal her completely. Elva is thrilled at the chance to get rid of the curse, and she doesn't really care whether healing her puts anyone else in danger or puts the Varden at risk (*Brisingr* pp. 262–263).

Although that might sound selfish, think about what she's been going through. Can you imagine what it must be like to feel the pain of every wound suffered by every soldier fighting in a battle? And that's just one example of what she has had to deal with every single day since Eragon supposedly blessed her. On top of that, she's also compelled to try to help everyone whose pain she feels, as the spell he cast requires her to shield everybody from hurt and pain or she becomes physically ill. Even worse is the fact that this started when she was an infant. Think what it would be like to just be coming into consciousness as a new life, and all of a sudden you can feel the pain of everyone around you!

Despite the fact that Eragon had given the problem careful consideration and come up with a spell that he thought would counter his initial blessing, it works only halfway. For after it's cast, Elva is still able to feel everybody around her. However, as Eragon is preparing to cast a second spell that might complete the first one, Elva makes an important discovery: she no longer is compelled to protect or help people. With the compulsion to shield everyone gone, she also realizes that she'll eventually be able to learn how to ignore what people are feeling because doing so won't cause her to be sick (*Brisingr* p. 267).

So instead of having Eragon search for a way to finish the job, she decides to keep her ability, for it also means she retains the ability to read people's fears. This fills her with malicious joy:

> *"[W]oe unto those who oppose me, for I know all*
> *their fears and shall not hesitate to play upon them*
> *in order to fulfill my wishes." (Brisingr* p. 268)

Eragon is aghast when he hears this and prepares to cast the counterspell without her permission, but she stops him before he can begin. The truth of her power is revealed at that moment. She is able to see into Eragon and read how much the memory of having forced a spell upon her would trouble him in the future:

> *"Every night when you lay yourself down to sleep,*
> *you will think of me, and the memory of the wrong*
> *you have committed will torment you." (Brisingr*
> p. 269)

As if it weren't bad enough that she was able to strike him dumb, her final words before leaving are even more chilling:

> "[W]hen, next we cross paths, Eragon Shadeslayer, count me not as a friend or foe. I am ambivalent toward you, Rider; I am just as prepared to hate you as I am to love you." (Brisingr p. 269)

Despite the fact that those words are somewhat softened by her avowal of love for Saphira, one can't help but think that Eragon has made an incredibly dangerous enemy. Even with Angela promising to try to educate and control her (Brisingr pp. 270), Elva will have to be considered a threat to Eragon unless something occurs to change her attitude toward him. The real danger with her is that she is so young and so gifted, with an incredible power to manipulate people's emotions in order to get whatever she wants. It's easy to forget, because she is so articulate, that she is actually little more than an infant and probably not much more emotionally sophisticated than one either.

Elva could bring new and awful meaning to the term *the terrible twos,* that stage of growth where children first become aware that they can think for themselves and start making demands on their parents. Most children at that stage have a tantrum when they can't get their way, not understanding that there are some things they just aren't allowed to do. It's at this point in their development that they begin to understand the difference between right and wrong, and they begin to understand the concept of responsibility. Can you imagine what shape one of Elva's tantrums would take if she couldn't get her way?

Elva: Power and Responsibility

Elva is a completely amoral creature, meaning she has no understanding of what's right and what's wrong. Everything revolves around what she wants and how she is going to be able to obtain that. Initially, her power to exploit a person's emotions was controlled by her compulsion to help that person, but now, with no such restriction placed on her, she is under no constraints when it comes to using her power. Although she chides Eragon for trying to impose his will upon her by casting a second spell without her permission (*Brisingr* p. 269), she is far more likely to abuse her power than he is.

The real question about Elva now is, What, if any, sort of threat does she pose to Eragon? Although Angela seems to be convinced that she herself is well protected against Elva's ability and will be able to control her in the long run, remember that when she cast Elva's fortune back in *Eldest*, it was a real quagmire, or, in other words, very confusing (*Eldest* p. 334). Angela also complains in *Brisingr* that she's going to have to spend the next decade teaching Elva how to behave (*Brisingr* p. 270). What's going to happen, though, in the meantime, before Elva has learned about the responsibilities that come with power?

It's probably unlikely that Eragon has to worry about the dagger in his ribs that Saphira makes a dark joke about (*Brisingr* p. 271). Nonetheless, there's still all sorts of other mischief that Elva could get into. Despite the fact that she could easily reveal to Galbatorix all of Eragon's innermost thoughts and fears—something that he would probably be able to take advantage of in one way or another—there's another, far more dangerous, risk that has to be considered. If Elva is able to read people's emotions so well that she can manipulate their behavior, doesn't it stand to reason that she could easily discover a person's true nature and, through that, his or her true name? What wouldn't Galbatorix give to know Eragon's true name!

Yes, it's true that Elva has said she will always love Saphira for marking her with the gedwëy ignasia and the blessing that accompanied it, but she doesn't seem to let her affection for Saphira interfere with her ambivalence about Eragon. It's more than likely that she wouldn't consider the implications that harming Eragon would have for Saphira if something moved her to act against him. A child will act without thinking about the consequences, so Elva might do just that. If you've ever seen a two-year-old or three-year-old act out, you'll not doubt the real danger she represents if she feels that Eragon is thwarting her in any way. She won't care what happens as a result of her actions, as she will be lashing out in a blind rage, no matter how calculating she appears to be.

Elva is not only a potential enemy, but one who has the power to harm Eragon in ways that nobody else can. It's the height of irony that the source of this creature's power is Eragon's accidental misuse of his own power. His real mistake was giving in to the demand of the old woman to bless the child in the first place, as he was too new to his powers at the time and his knowledge of the ancient tongue too imperfect. It was irresponsible on his part to attempt a blessing without even consulting anyone with more knowledge of the language.

The character of Elva is important to the plot of the book not only because of her potential for danger to Eragon and the

Varden, but because she helps to emphasize Paolini's theme that power needs to be accompanied by a sense of responsibility. For Eragon, she will be a constant reminder of that fact, as he is responsible for her condition and thus indirectly responsible for any damage she might cause. Elva, unlike Eragon, appears to have no compunction about using her power for whatever suits her needs, and is a perfect example of what happens when power is exercised carelessly. We've already seen Elva breach Eragon's and her caregiver's defenses without a qualm, and these are two people who have at least been trying to help her. I dread to think what would happen to someone who actually tried to deny Elva her heart's desire!

Amid all the other dangers that he will have to face in Book Four, it looks as though Eragon will also have to be watching his back, keeping a careful eye on Elva. Although it's hard to predict exactly what she will do, or if she will even do anything at all, just the fact that she's potentially a danger will be sufficient to force Eragon to commit scarce resources to ensuring she isn't able to harm him. Of course, there's still the chance that she could use her powers to help Eragon and Saphira, if the mood strikes her. And she could prove invaluable in any direct conflict with Galbatorix because she can anticipate a person's actions based on their emotional state. Which side of that coin turns up depends on her attitude. Will she use her power selfishly? Or will she use her abilities to help others? Either way, she's bound to make her presence felt before Book Four is over. Let's just hope she uses her power for good, not evil, or things could get messy.

Chapter 13

Shades and Spirits

Magic! More people have probably written about, fantasized about, and dreamed about it than nearly any other subject around. And why not? Who wouldn't want to have the power to do things just by waving a wand or speaking an incantation? Of course, magic has a rather shady reputation in our society, with people at various times associating it with evil powers and proclaiming its use a sign of ungodliness and other superstitious nonsense, but that hasn't prevented the rest of us from being fascinated by it. I'll bet that you have wished, at one time or another, that you could perform some sort of magic. I know I have.

We've already seen how magic in Alagaësia depends on knowledge of a specific language and the ability to use it to describe what you want something or someone to do. However, it requires more than just knowledge of the language to be able to perform magic. It also requires the expenditure of a great deal of energy. A young spellcaster like Eragon has only a limited amount of power stored within his body, which quickly becomes exhausted after casting only a few spells. Look at what happens to him when he uses magic for the first time. He sends an arrow of blue flame at some attacking Urgals and then collapses (*Eragon* p. 134). Without an external source of energy, or something to draw upon to replenish their own stores, a spellcaster could be left defenseless or even die by casting too many spells or by attempting one that's too powerful.

To overcome this problem, most spellcasters carry with them objects that they have stored energy in, which they can draw upon in the heat of battle. The drawback to this—as we saw with Oromis when he lost his sword, Naegling, which he and Glaedr had invested with energy during his battle with Murtagh and Thorn (*Brisingr* p. 734)—is if the spellcaster becomes separated from the object, they are left without the means to power their spells.

Of course, a Dragon Rider has other means at their disposal, every bit as effective, for drawing upon external sources of energy. Due to their unique bond, a Rider is always able to draw upon the power of their dragon in order to bolster their own reserves. And a Rider isn't limited to just their dragon. A Dragon Rider can also link with any number of other spellcasters and make use of their energy supply, as Eragon does with his elvish bodyguard and Arya during his second battle with Murtagh (*Brisingr* pp. 316–329). But neither a Rider's dragon nor other spellcasters are a limitless supply of energy, and a careless Rider could either injure or kill them by draining them dry. Of course, a Dragon Rider in possession of another Rider's dragon's Eldunarí, "heart of hearts," is able to draw upon its energy to bolster their resources, even if that dragon isn't around. However, I would assume that in order for the Rider to be able to make use of the Eldunarí, they would have to keep it with them, so the same risk applies to it as with any other object.

There is also a way for a spellcaster to draw energy from the world around them, but at such a dreadful cost that the magic user would either have to be desperate or evil to make use of it. They can literally draw upon the life force of other living creatures for energy to restore any that they have lost. In the process, however, they kill whatever they have drawn upon. Eragon was forced to make use of this method during his escape with Sloan in *Brisingr* (pp. 69–70). As he pulled energy from around him, he watched as shrubs and plants withered and died in order to feed him. Having learned from the elves to respect the sanctity of all life, he is sickened by the results. The only reason he used that method at the time was because it was a matter of life and death; it's not something he's going to be in a rush to do again.

However, the magic used by Dragon Riders is only one type of magic that exists in Alagaësia, for witches and wizards, sorcerers, and, most deadly of all, Shades live there, too. Although witches and wizards draw upon potions and specific spells for their power, sorcerers and Shades utilize the power of spirits to accomplish their will. As with Dragon Riders, the power of witches and wizards is neither good nor evil; it can be used for either purpose. The same applies to sorcerers, for despite the fact that their magic relies on binding spirits to their service, it does not dictate their intent or their character. In fact, the leader of the Varden's spellcasters, Trianna, is a sorcerer, and she has dedicated herself to the overthrow of Galbatorix. However, although sorcerers merely use their magical strength to control spirits and the spirits' powers, Shades relinquish their control, allowing spirits to control their bodies. As only the most evil of spirits are interested in controlling a human, those magic users who become Shades, whether it was their intention or not, become evil and can be incredibly destructive. It was Angela who explained this difference to Eragon, after he told her about Durza. At the time, she said that aside from Galbatorix, Durza represented the greatest threat to the Varden (*Eragon* pp. 437).

Remember how, in his battle with Durza, Eragon managed to break into the Shade's mind, experience his memories, and learn his history? Durza was originally only a sorcerer, but called upon spirits that were too strong and powerful for him to control, which resulted in him being turned into a Shade. Those memories were so powerful that even after Durza's death, they threatened to overwhelm Eragon. It was only through the timely intervention of Oromis, contacting him from afar through his mind, that he was able to garner the strength required to overcome the malevolence of the spirits that had been transferred to him while he was in Durza's mind (*Eragon* pp. 493–494). Needless to say, this rather limited exposure to spirits didn't leave Eragon with the most favorable of impressions.

So the confusion he feels when he and Arya encounter spirits while traveling together on his return to the Varden after his rescue of Katrina is understandable (*Brisingr* pp. 210–215). For when one of the spirits entered his awareness, it left him feeling positively ecstatic. Yet no matter how good it made him feel, its presence within felt so alien that he wanted nothing more than to escape from it. However, he was unable to do so; it had completely taken over his consciousness. If the spirit had desired, it could have possessed him as easily as those who had taken over Durza. Instead, it merely examined him, learned all it could about him, and then departed. Eragon was left with a sense of regret, missing the great bliss with which the spirit had filled him during the time it controlled him.

Nobody knows much about spirits, not even elves. What they do know is what they aren't; they know that neither humans nor elves nor dwarves nor any other creatures become these spirits after they die. They are not ghosts. Part of the problem is that spirits have so little in common with the rest of the races of Alagaësia that it's almost impossible to communicate with them. Nor can you ever be sure how they're going to react when you meet them. They appear to be so powerful that it doesn't look like anybody has any real defenses against them. Seemingly, all that stands in the way of them taking over people whenever they feel like it is that they hate the feeling of confinement. In fact, as Arya explains to Eragon after their encounter with them, that's one of the reasons they do their best to induce a sense of rapture in anybody they encounter. They figure that if they make people happy, they are less liable to try to control them, although after what

Eragon experienced, it seems as though anybody trying to control a spirit stands as good a chance of being controlled as they do of being in charge. Once a spirit has occupied a person's consciousness, they look to be as difficult to remove as a leech and as hard to control as the weather.

Now, aside from being the source for another form of magic, one that has the potential for giving its practitioner a great deal of power, there's something about spirits that must be important to the outcome of the battle for Alagaësia. Otherwise, Christopher Paolini wouldn't have had Eragon and Arya have that encounter with them in *Brisingr*. He wouldn't have made such a big deal of them or raised the question about who they were originally. Although it's true that Arya and Eragon encounter a Shade again at the end of *Brisingr* (p. 736), readers already know enough about Shades from the encounter with Durza to understand the danger they represent. So there has to be another reason for supplying additional information about spirits. Aside from their potential danger as Shades, what other role could spirits play in determining the outcome of the series?

The first thing to try to figure out is who these spirits are exactly, as we know who they aren't. Think back to what Oromis told Eragon about the mysterious Grey Folk. When magic ran wild throughout the land, they were the ones to devise a way to control it by binding it to their language. Then, once they cast that spell, their civilization dwindled, as some intermarried with other races until they were no longer distinct, while others simply "faded away" (*Eldest* p. 399). It's almost as if the casting of the spell used them up as a people.

What happened to those members of the population who faded away? Did they just disappear into thin air? What if those who chose to fade away didn't simply vanish, as is thought, but changed the nature of their existence? Although the spell they cast may have required such enormous amounts of energy that they were too exhausted to go on as they were, what would have prevented them from continuing to exist, but in a different manner, on a less tangible plane?

Of course, does it really matter whom these spirits are if they can't be communicated with and all they seem interested in is self-preservation? Even if they are what's left of the Grey Folk, why would they care what happens to the living of Alagaësia? Would it make any difference to them who rules? Although on the surface they might not seem to care, and they appear to be so powerful that they don't need to worry about anything that the other life forms worry about, remember how much they hate and fear being held captive. They turned the tables on Durza when he summoned them, transforming him into an evil creature bent on destruction. But when Arya told the spirits whom she and Eragon encountered that he had freed those spirits captured by Durza, they were so pleased that they gave them a gift—a living lily made from gold (*Brisingr* p. 216).

It seems that spirits share a collective consciousness, so that when something happens to one, they are all aware of it. How else could you explain why the spirits Arya and Eragon met knew about the spirits he freed when he killed Durza? If that's the case, there's a good chance they would be willing to help somebody who made the effort to free spirits who were similarly trapped and would oppose anybody who made use of captured spirits. Of course, the problem of how to communicate with them remains. Although they are attracted to magic, it appears that using magic around spirits can put you in mortal danger. Remember, Arya warned Eragon not to use magic when she first detected their presence. So that doesn't appear to be the most helpful or intelligent way to attract their attention.

However, there might be another way. Think back to the mysterious advice given by Solembum the first time Eragon met the werecat. We know that his advice is good because it's already resulted in Eragon receiving the weapon he required, but nobody has yet to understand the second bit: *"Then, when all seems lost and your power is insufficient, go to the Rock of Kuthian and speak your name to open the Vault of Souls"* (*Eragon* p. 206). Everyone whom Eragon has repeated those words to has been at a loss to explain them. Although Oromis says that he has heard of the Rock of Kuthian, he can't remember where, and he has no idea what the Vault of Souls is (*Brisingr* p. 639). Of course, it's possible that both locations have something to do with the Eldunarí, but they could both have something to do with spirits, who float at will throughout Alagaësia.

Oromis and Glaedr spent decades searching for any other hoard of Eldunarí—for any sign that any might exist outside the king's control—and came up empty-handed (*Brisingr* p. 636). Therefore, there's a really good chance that the Vault of Souls has something to do with the Grey Folk. It strikes me as too much of a coincidence that little is known about spirits and hardly anything is known about the Vault of Souls; my intuition says that there is a connection between the two.

Think of the power that a sorcerer with only a few spirits under his or her control is able to summon; at the end of *Brisingr*, it takes the combined strength of Arya, Eragon, and Saphira to overcome one sorcerer who controls just a few spirits (pp. 736–738). What kind of strength would Eragon have at his command if he could make an arrangement with the spirits of the Grey Folk? Galbatorix? Heck, nobody would stand a chance against Eragon. Even the risk of working with spirits doesn't need to be a factor in gaining access to their power. Eragon wouldn't be seeking to control them. He'd merely be asking them for assistance in ridding the world of Galbatorix, somebody who would, given half a chance, enslave them. True, there is the difficulty involved in trying to communicate anything at all to spirits. But Arya was able to let them know that Eragon had freed the spirits trapped by Durza, so there must be some way of letting them know his intent. They might even be feeling somewhat beholden to him, because he's freed spirits from the control of a Shade twice. Judging by the gift they gave him and Arya, they are capable of showing appreciation, and therefore could prove to be willing partners.

We know that spirits aren't ghosts of any creatures that have lived, so that precludes them from being related to any of the sentient beings now alive in Alagaësia. But the Grey Folk never really died. They just vanished after casting the one great spell needed to give their language the power to control magic. Who's to say that these beings of pure power aren't all that's left of the first race of beings who lived in Alagaësia?

They sacrificed themselves thousands of years ago in order to make the world safe from the danger of uncontrolled magic, so Galbatorix would be an abomination in their eyes. If ever there was an example of the world needing to be kept safe from someone who misuses magic, he is it.

They've already scanned Eragon and have an understanding of who he is and what he stands for. In all probability, they've even learned his true name ("*[S]peak your name to open the Vault of Souls*") (*Eragon* p. 206) and would recognize him if he came calling. This means that he has a far better chance than anybody else does of convincing them to become allies. Before the war is over, the spirits of Alagaësia are going to play a significant role in events. The chances of them being behind the mystery of what's contained in the Vault of Souls seem more than good to me. Wouldn't it be fitting if the first people of Alagaësia, the mysterious Grey Folk, came out of the past to help the namesake of the first Dragon Rider defeat the greatest threat the world has known since they gave up their physical form?

With Galbatorix having a firm grasp on almost all the Eldunarí in existence, it makes sense for Eragon to search for an alternative magic to assist him in his forthcoming battle with the king. Even if he can't cut the king off from the power of the hearts of hearts, having a source of power as strong as the spirits would make him possibly more powerful than any spellcaster that he would meet in the field of battle — including Galbatorix.

Chapter 14

The Wild Cards

As in any series, the Inheritance cycle includes a variety of secondary characters who, despite the fact that they're not as important to the outcome of the story as the leads, can still play a significant role. Whether their actions directly affect the main characters or they serve as the catalyst for other events, something happens because of their actions, and the ripples of turbulence caused by their behavior can spread far and wide. Like the joker in a deck of cards that turns up to foil your plans, these wild cards can cause more trouble than you might think possible. Think about the impact that Sloan's actions had on the entire village of Carvahall, or what happened because of the Twins' treachery, and you'll have a pretty good idea of what I'm talking about.

Now, these characters can't be so minor that we barely notice them, but they aren't people who make appearances as frequently as Roran or Eragon, or are as important to the plot as Murtagh or Oromis. No, these wild cards are Angela, Queen Islanzadí of the elves, or Jeod, characters who make occasional but important appearances throughout. Sometimes you aren't even aware of the significance of the character's contribution at the moment. But at some point in the story, they, or something they've done, will either benefit or harm the lead character, or push the story in an unexpected direction. There have already been instances of this happening in the Inheritance cycle. And some of the secondary characters could still end up playing a role in how things turn out in the end. They may not be the reason that Galbatorix is overthrown, but they could make the job either easier or more difficult. Which of the cast of thousands still have something left to contribute, or are lurking in the wings, just waiting for their moment to jump out and surprise us all?

The villagers of Carvahall are almost universal in their admiration of Roran for the way he was able to, pretty much through the force of his will, lead them across the country — out of Galbatorix's clutches to the relative safety of life among the Varden. But at least one among them holds a grudge against him. Birgit holds Roran responsible for the death of her husband, who was killed during attempts by the Ra'zac and soldiers of the Empire to capture him before the villagers made their escape and become refugees. So intense was her grief that she swore an oath: one way or another, he would compensate her for the loss of her husband (*Eldest* p. 261). However, she also knows that Roran represents her best hope of both escaping the Empire and balancing the scales with the

Ra'zac, who killed her mate. So she's willing to bide her time until both of their primary goals are met: making sure the village makes it safely to the Varden and the Ra'zac have been brought to justice.

Time and again throughout the journey across Alagaësia, she proves herself to be as tough as any of the men. She is one of the people Roran comes to count on the most during the journey, knowing that she will do whatever is necessary without complaint or hesitation. It's Birgit who distracts the men guarding the *Dragon Wing*, the ship they steal in order to make the journey from Teirm to Surda and the Varden (*Eldest* p. 510). However, she also never lets an opportunity pass to remind Roran of her intention. Someday, she will exact her price from him for the death of her husband. Even once they have made it safely to the Varden's camp, she hasn't forgiven or forgotten her vow. She makes this perfectly clear when Roran returns from rescuing Katrina and brings back news that the Ra'zac and their parents are dead:

> *"And do you remember I promised that once the Ra'zac were dead, I would have my compensation from you for your role in Quimby's death....I would not want your memory to fail you. I will have my compensation, Garrowsson. Never you doubt that."*
> (*Brisingr* p. 156)

Although Roran knows full well that she's not making idle threats, she seems to be going about seeking compensation in a very odd manner. For, aside from the occasion when she made the preceding speech — prior to which Roran had caught her eyeing him with a knife in her hands — she has made no move against him. In fact, her actions seem to contradict her vow. When Roran and Katrina are married, it's Birgit who speaks for Katrina, because Katrina's mother is dead and her father is (supposedly) dead. She accepts Roran's offer of what he brings to their marriage on her behalf and itemizes Katrina's dowry in exchange (*Brisingr* p. 344). Before the wedding, she took part in making the feast and the (equally important) friendly teasing of the groom. Although her behavior may be explained away because she was a close friend of Katrina's late mother, her actions are still far from being the actions of a person hell bent on revenge. Yet that doesn't prevent Roran from believing that a day of reckoning will come, and fear her potential to do him harm.

Nothing further has happened between Birgit and Roran by the time that *Brisingr* comes to an end. She's obviously willing to wait for Galbatorix to be overthrown before she exacts her payment. The one thing we can be sure of is that, unlike others—Sloan, for instance—Birgit won't turn Roran over to the Empire in order to take her vengeance. Despite the fact that she holds him responsible for the circumstances that brought about her husband's death, she gives the king and his forces an equal share of the blame. After all, it wasn't Roran who actually killed her husband, it was Galbatorix's servants. Yet Christopher Paolini wouldn't keep reminding us of her intentions if he didn't mean for them to be significant, so we have to consider Birgit's threat against Roran a serious one. The easiest way to get at Roran would be an attack on Katrina, of course, but Birgit has already proven her loyalty to her by standing up with her at the wedding. Anyway, that's not Birgit's style. She seems to be someone who will either confront you directly or not all. Obviously, she can challenge him to a fight and try to kill him. This might have been her original plan, but it probably no longer seems like such a good idea, because Roran has become a formidable fighter since joining the Varden.

Of course, if she did challenge him, there's always the possibility that he might only defend himself, leaving himself open to being injured or even killed. However, what is more likely is that she'll seek some other form of compensation. As a widow with children, she will be hard pressed to provide her kids with an inheritance. So she could demand that Roran surrender the farm land that he inherited from Gowan as reparation. Although Roran might be dismayed by the loss of his family's farm, he wouldn't have any way of denying Birgit her demand without fighting her, which is what he wants to avoid.

Without land, Roran and Katrina will be forced to change their plans after the war, because obviously he won't be able to return to Carvahall as a farmer if he doesn't have any land to work. He's going to have to put some of his new skills as a warrior and leader to use if he wants to provide for his family. This means that he will be ideally situated to take a position of authority in the new government of Alagaësia after the war. Can you think of a better person to be, say, the new governor of any territory where the Urgals settle after the war? If Roran had his father's land to go back to, he would probably turn down any offers of leadership in the new government. But perhaps, thanks to Birgit, he will be able to live up to his potential and offer his wife and family a security that a farmer could only dream of.

That may sound a little far-fetched. But it would not only resolve the Birgit issue nicely, it would also allow everything to work out for the best for the lead characters, which is just one way an author can put his unpredictable and volatile wild cards to good use. The intentions of the wild cards aren't always going to be positive, but that doesn't prevent what they do from having a positive outcome.

On the other hand, not all the wild card characters are as benign as Birgit probably is; in fact, some are downright deadly. Early on, when Eragon is among the dwarves, he discovers, through his conversation with King Hrothgar, that more than a few dwarves are not only against fighting alongside the Varden, but are violently opposed to himself and to Dragon Riders (*Eragon* p. 441). They figure that if they had ignored the world and hadn't helped the Riders in the first place, Galbatorix and company would have left them alone. So now they want to turn their backs on the world.

Most of those opposed to working with the Varden end up obeying their king and the majority opinion, but the members of one clan, Az Sweldn rak Anhûin. (The Tears of Anhûin), aren't content with making their displeasure known through their words. They are willing to resort to violence to get their way, as they show when they try to assassinate Eragon during the sessions to elect the new dwarf king (*Brisingr* pp. 450–455). Fortunately, not only does their plan to kill Eragon fail, but their intent backfires, as it ensures the election of Eragon and Nasuada's adoptive clan brother, Orik, as the new king (*Brisingr*

p. 543). On the surface, this looks like another instance of wild card characters' activities turning out for the best, in spite of themselves. Unfortunately, their clan leader is shunned by the rest of the dwarves, and the clan itself is shunned until they replace him and apologize for their actions (*Brisingr* p. 501), making them more isolated than ever. Although this may cause them to reconsider their position and attitude, it could also end up pushing them to take even more drastic action.

Az Swelden rak Anhûin is not the traditional name of the clan, and the reason behind their new name helps to explain their animosity toward Eragon and Dragon Riders in general. Before the time of Galbatorix, they had been one of the richest dwarf clans and their members were some of the staunchest supporters of the Riders. Unfortunately for them, not only had they volunteered their greatest warriors in service to the Riders, they also lived in a very exposed part of the dwarf kingdom. After Galbatorix overthrew the Riders' city of Urû'baen, he and the Forsworn attacked the dwarves, and their clan paid the heaviest price, with only their leader, Anhûin, and her guards surviving the onslaught.

After she died of grief, her followers took the name Az Swelden rak Anhûin, The Tears of Anhûin, and covered their faces in veils as a permanent reminder of their grief and their thirst for revenge (*Eldest* p. 109). But they have been blinded by their desire for vengeance, and are unable to discern the difference between a Rider such as Eragon and the Riders of the Forsworn. To them, he is a reminder of the horrors they suffered and is as much their enemy as if he had been one of those who killed their brothers and sisters all those years ago.

How far would they be willing to go for revenge? Now that they are shunned, they might even consider forming an alliance with Galbatorix to ensure the survival of their little community, even if the rest of the dwarves were destroyed. Remember, Galbatorix can be very convincing when he wants to, sweetening his words so much that he even attempts to fool Oromis in *Brisingr* (p. 732). It might not be difficult for him to convince the Az Sweldn rak Anhûin, blinkered by their selfishness and anger, that if they work for him, he will give them anything they want. Because they are considered pariahs by the rest of the dwarves, the more fanatical elements among them might well consider any action justified if it gives them vengeance against the rest of the clans. As their clan chief, Vermûnd, spouts after the Council of Elders banishes him and his clan, they are the only "true" dwarves (*Brisingr* p. 501). They've already proven their willingness to kill their own kind before, so what's to prevent them from attempting to, say, assassinate Orik in order to sow turmoil among the clans?

Can you imagine the chaos if Orik were killed just before the ultimate battle between the Varden and the Empire? What if Az Swelden rak Anhûin were able to cast suspicion for his death on the Urgals or even just another dwarf clan who opposed the war? If Galbatorix's armies were able to time an attack upon the Varden to coincide with the confusion that such an event would guarantee, they could deliver a defeat that ended the rebellion permanently. Without the dwarves fighting alongside them, the Varden would not only be vastly outnumbered, they would be horribly dispirited.

Although that's an extreme example of the type of damage Az Swelden rak Anhûin could inflict, they could do other things to harm the war effort and earn the favor of Galbatorix. They could attack an Urgal encampment and make it look like the work of another dwarf clan, causing the already fragile alliance to splinter. They could even join forces with Galbatorix and fight with his army against their own people, which would dismay Orik's people. They could create special difficulties if they were to ditch their veils, insinuate themselves into Orik's troops, and, during the battle, start attacking the Varden from behind their own lines.

Sound unlikely? Remember that when he was shunned, the clan leader threatened to make war on the rest of the clans if they took any action against his clan for trying to assassinate Eragon (*Brisingr* p. 499). When they elected to shun him instead, he rained curses down upon their heads, until he and his followers stormed out of the meeting hall. They do not seem like the type of people who are going to take this lying down. More than likely, they will attempt something in order to pay back this insult to their clan. They can make some serious mischief for the Varden, and we shouldn't be surprised to see them make some move or other before the series is over. This move could cause irreparable harm, perhaps even result in the death of somebody dear to Eragon.

The other characters who represent something of a wild card are the Urgals. Not only is their behavior unpredictable, but they are barely tolerated by their allies. Just prior to the battle of the Burning Plains in *Eldest* (p. 609), Nasuada accepts the offer of more than eight hundred Kull, the warrior caste of the Urgals, to fight alongside the Varden against the king. Galbatorix betrayed them by offering them land in exchange for fighting alongside Durza, but then Durza forced them to do things they didn't want to do and enslaved them. When Durza was defeated, Galbatorix reneged on his offer of land to the Urgals and abandoned them. Naturally, many among the Varden, including Eragon initially, resist the idea of having the Urgals as allies, for many of them have fought them in the past and seen family and friends killed by them. However, Nasuada's argument — she lost her father to them but is willing to fight alongside them — is hard for anybody to counter, so their presence is grudgingly accepted.

That doesn't prevent problems, as is seen in *Brisingr* (p. 576), when Nasuada asks Roran to lead a mixed company of humans and Urgals, hoping that he can keep the alliance together after a human slipped into the Urgal encampment and killed three of them. Despite the fact that she quickly had the culprit hung, Nasuada is rightly worried that if this sort of dissension continues, she could have a war among her own troops on her hands. Although Roran is able to win over the Urgals in his war party by defeating the one who challenges him for leadership of the war band in single, unarmed combat, the matter is by no means settled. Far too much bad blood still exists between Urgals and humans, Urgals and dwarves, and Urgals and elves for the resentment that's built up between species to be smoothed over easily. Although it may not be the Urgals themselves who cause problems, the mere fact that they are around could lead to trouble for the Varden.

A foe like Galbatorix will always be on the lookout for a way to weaken his opponent without having to expend any of his own resources. And what better way of doing that than spreading disunity among them? Az Swelden rak Anhûin are one means at his disposal for doing that, but I'm certain that he'd be more than willing to make use of any people's prejudices and bigotry to serve his purposes. All he need do is arrange something simple, such as making it look as though an Urgal killed a human child and ate it, to see the Varden tearing itself to pieces. An experienced magic user could easily plant that suggestion in a susceptible human's brain. The rumor would spread like wildfire among the humans, leading to anything from an investigation to a full-scale riot if the humans took it upon themselves to attack the Urgal camp.

These scenarios aren't hard to imagine, for not only does the king have the means at his disposal to set them in motion, far too many people would be willing to believe their prejudices over anything else. It has to be hoped that nothing like this happens, but the very unpredictability of the whole situation makes trouble of some sort or another predictable. Thankfully, the presence of Eragon and Saphira will help to deter the most extreme violence, but this sort of situation could still result in the loss of lives or, even worse, disunity among the Varden. The Urgals are a valuable ally to have in a battle, as they are fierce creatures. But in the end, they could be the cause of some sort of trouble that will end up making the task of overthrowing the king that much more difficult.

Birgit, Az Swelden rak Anhûin, and the Urgals aren't major characters in the series, but they, along with Sloan and Elva, will have something to say regarding the final outcome of the story. They may not directly affect the outcome of the war, but they could alter the fate of a major character through their actions. Certainly, other characters pop up throughout the story, but these are the ones most likely to influence the course of events in the final book. At the very least, their actions to date mean that we should keep an eye on them—just in case. We can only hope that, no matter what their intent, something positive will come about because of their actions, or that the cost involved in overcoming their actions isn't too steep.

Chapter 15

What About...?

Like all good authors, Christopher Paolini has scattered bits of information throughout the series that suggest what might be forthcoming. These elements of foreshadowing are either tantalizing hints about the future or clues about the riddles that characters need to solve. Some are direct in their meaning, for instance, Angela's fortunetelling (*Eragon* pp. 203–206). And others, such as the advice given to Eragon by Angela's companion, Solembum the werecat, in the same chapter, are more obscure. Sometimes these hints or clues come in the form of snippets of dialogue overheard, or pieces of information that are idly dropped in conversation that, at the time, seem insignificant, but could later be of incredible importance.

Now, quite a number of these little tidbits have already come to fruition—Eragon did find what he needed at the base of the Menoa tree for a weapon, as Solembum said he would

(*Eragon* p. 206). And, as Angela predicted, a family member has betrayed him, although there still could be more to that prediction. We've already tried to figure out the conundrum behind the second part of Solembum's cryptic advice. And we've tried to unravel the mystery of exactly what the Ra'zac meant when, in his final moments before Eragon killed him, he said that Galbatorix had almost found the true name of somebody or something (*Brisingr* p. 65). However, there are still plenty of those little mysteries floating around that could be significant. Of course, there's always the chance of reading too much into every last little thing that is said, overheard, or thought by the various characters. But when you're looking for answers to things that are so puzzling that sometimes you don't even know the right question to ask, you can't afford to let anything slip by. Even the trivial conversation between two soldiers that Eragon overhears on his way back to the Varden—after he has killed the Ra'zac and Galbatorix has mobilized nearly his entire army in an attempt to find him— could be significant. They are complaining about the dangers of searching for whatever killed the Ra'zac and are wondering why the king isn't using Murtagh and Thorn to search for them, when one soldier says, "Unless we be searching for Murtagh....You heard what Morzan's spawn said well as I did" (*Brisingr* pp. 129–130).

Eragon's first thought is to try to maintain the spell keeping the soldiers from spotting him. But after he's safe from discovery, all he can think of is what it was Murtagh could have said to cause that reaction from the king's men.

Obviously, it must have been something treasonous or else the one guard wouldn't have suggested they were out hunting Murtagh. So it's only natural that Eragon is intrigued. He'd give anything to know that his former friend — the man he thinks is his brother — is doing everything he can to resist Galbatorix. Unfortunately, as he's soon to find out, whatever it was that Murtagh said, it doesn't mean that he's putting up much resistance to the king. For when they meet only a few chapters later in the book, Murtagh is still bound and determined to haul Eragon and Saphira back with him as prisoners. He would have succeeded this time, too, if it weren't for the help Eragon received from the twelve elvish spellcasters and Arya during the battle (*Brisingr* pp. 316–329). So whatever thoughts Murtagh expressed that riled up the soldiers, or that Galbatorix considered treasonous, they were spoken in the heat of anger. Or else they were trampled out of him by the king, who was reinforcing his control over him by forcing him to swear more oaths binding him to the throne. After Murtagh's aforementioned battle with Eragon, and his killing of Oromis (*Brisingr* p. 734), the chances of Murtagh breaking free of the king's control, or even attempting to overcome the spells that are holding him in place, are fading fast. No matter how much hope Eragon might have taken from that snippet of conversation, it's doubtful that there is any real significance to it. Unfortunately, Murtagh is lost. And it doesn't look as though he's going to be able to find his way to redemption in time to save himself.

On the other hand, something that could be significant happens during Eragon's last stay among the elves. This incident, which could be missed if the reader isn't paying careful attention, could play a key role in determining Eragon's future. The Menoa tree has just given up the brightsteel buried beneath her roots that is required to make Eragon's sword when:

> *Eragon felt a slight twinge in his lower belly. He winced and rubbed at the spot, but the momentary flare of discomfort had already vanished. (Brisingr p. 659)*

Don't feel too bad if you didn't notice what the tree takes as payment for the brightsteel on your first reading of the text. Eragon himself doesn't associate the slight stab of pain in his lower abdomen with payment of the debt he owes the tree. He even persists in trying to ask the tree what she wants, but as her consciousness retreats from his, he realizes she's not about to tell him. What sort of price could a tree exact from a human? To answer that, we have to take a closer look at exactly who the Menoa tree is. From that, we might be able to figure out what she took and what it might mean for Eragon in the long run.

Back in *Eldest*, Arya told Eragon the story of Linnëa, an older elf, and how she had murdered a young man who had been her lover and then left her for a younger woman. Knowing that she had done wrong, she lost her joy for life and went into the depths of the forest until she came to the oldest tree in the woods. Pressing herself against it, she sang herself into the tree, surrendering herself to it and relinquishing her association with the outside world. After three days and three nights of singing, she had become one with the tree, and ever since then, for thousands of years, she has kept watch over the forest as the Menoa tree (*Eldest* p. 307). When Arya first took Eragon to see the tree, he had reached out with his consciousness to feel all the living things around him, and was shocked to discover that it was not only awake, but intelligent.

So somewhere deep within the tree rests the awareness of an elf woman, but these days her main concerns are those of a growing creature, and she has little care for the business of elves and humans. In fact, the only way that Eragon and Saphira are able to get her attention when they want to ask her about Solembum's advice, is by Saphira striking her and threatening her with fire. Naturally, her reaction to being attacked is to fight back, and such is her power that she could have easily killed both of them. All that saves them is her curiosity over just what Eragon is—the changes that he had undergone at the hands of the dragons during the Blood-oath Celebration made him unrecognizable, as far as she was concerned—and the promise of being given whatever she wants in return for the brightsteel (*Brisingr* pp. 657–659).

What could the Menoa tree have taken from him that seemed so insignificant to Eragon that he barely noticed it happening, but was enough to satisfy her? Obviously, she took something from his body, something that she desired or needed. Thinking back to her history, and what happened to her when she was still an elf, you can't help but wonder if it had something to do with Eragon being a young man, and she's done something to ensure that he's going to be forever loyal to her, unlike another young man, who deserted her. That's not to say that she's going to make him become a tree and join her on that level, but it could mean that she's taken something from him that will ensure that he is tied to Du Weldenvarden and its forest. He is destined to be exiled from Alagaësia, remember, and although it's been said that he will end up taking Oromis's place as the one to instruct new Dragon Riders, he wouldn't have to move to the elf kingdom in order to carry out his new duties. The piece that the Menoa tree has taken from him could be what forces him to spend the rest of his days tied to the forest as its guardian, and, by extension, the elf kingdom as well.

Of all the mysterious beings that Eragon meets on his travels throughout the human, dwarf, and elf kingdoms, one of the oddest is the pure white raven, Blagden, whom he meets upon first arriving in Ellesméra (*Eldest* p. 231). Part court jester, part sage, Blagden was given the power of speech by Arya's father as a reward for saving his life in battle. Somehow, the act also changed the bird's plumage from its natural black to pure white. In our world, the raven is a powerful figure in cultures as diverse as the old Norse tradition and the Native American tradition. In Norse mythology, Odin uses two ravens, Thought (Huginn) and Memory (Muninn), to help him see what is going on in the world and predict what will happen over the course of a day. (See the Wikipedia Web site at http://en.wikipedia.org/wiki/Hugin_and_Munin for information on the subject.) In the Native American tradition, the raven can be both a trickster and a creator. (For more information on ravens in Native American traditions, see the Godchecker Web site at http://www.godchecker.com/pantheon/native_american-mythology.php?deity=RAVEN.) Trickster figures in the Native American tradition are those whose actions run contrary to the way people normally behave; their misadventures are used as lessons for teaching the proper way of doing things. Tricksters are also those whose actions seem to be purposeless or foolish, but are really a disguise for wisdom. Our good friend Blagden looks to be a combination of both traditions, as he seems to embody characteristics of both the fool *and* the sage. He occasionally spouts bits of nonsensical, even insulting, poetry as well as occasionally offers riddles that predict the future.

The first time we meet him, he offers this rude piece of doggerel to Saphira: "Dragons, like wagons, / Have tongues. / Dragons, like flagons, / Have necks. / But while two hold beer, / The other eats deer!" (*Eldest* p. 235). Utter nonsense on the surface, but you might remember an instance when a certain dragon managed to get quite drunk when she drank far too much mead while visiting the dwarves (*Eldest* p. 51). This rhyme could be Blagden's not-so-gentle way of letting Saphira know that he's well aware of the time she made a fool of herself. For that's something else tricksters do for people: deflate their egos by reminding them of their mistakes and how they are less than perfect. Of course, it's hard to know when you should take Blagden's announcements seriously. Arya tells Eragon that he should take the raven seriously if he isn't speaking in verse; there could be wisdom lurking beneath his apparent foolishness (*Eldest* p. 236).

It's of some significance that three of the times that Eragon hears Blagden speak are when he is under the Menoa tree. On the first of those occasions, Arya is just about to recount the story of how Linnëa joined herself to the tree when, from his perch in the tree's branches, Blagden croaks out "Wyrda," the word for "fate" in the ancient language (*Eldest* p. 306). Although this could be taken as a commentary on the story and the strange things that can happen in life, he repeats his earlier remark a short while later. This time, he utters the word after Eragon has finished explaining to Arya how he had unintentionally cursed Elva when he misused the word for *shield* in attempting to bless her. It's just as Eragon has finished saying, "I only wonder what will become of the child" that Blagden repeats his earlier cry, "Wyrda" (*Eldest* p. 310). The fact that he's bracketed the two stories with his proclamation about fate is chilling; it implies that this was meant to be, that no matter what Eragon's intent, nothing can be done. And although Eragon does try to correct his mistake, he is unable to completely mend his original spell, and Elva elects to retain her power to manipulate others through her awareness of their innermost thoughts and emotions.

The third time that Blagden cries "Wyrda" for Eragon is just prior to the dance performed by the two elves known as the Caretakers, Iduna and Nëya. This occurs during the closing ceremonies of the Blood-oath Celebration, which honors the treaty between the elves and dragons that gave rise to the first Dragon Riders. Again, fate intervenes to change someone's life in a drastic manner; this time, it is Eragon's. A tattoo of a dragon, which covers the bodies of the two elves, is brought to life by the magic of the dance. It not only heals him of the damage inflicted on him by Durza, but physically transforms him, so that he has the powers of an elf (*Eldest* p. 471).

Although it might seem that fate has been cruel to Linnëa and Elva, and kind to Eragon, perhaps the real message is that the twists and turns of life have actually helped each of the three fulfill their destinies. For if Eragon hadn't been injured by Durza, would this transformation have taken place? And some might see it as a curse to be in either Elva's or Linnëa's position, but both end up choosing to be who they already are. It is a lesson that Eragon would do well to heed in the coming days, to not judge what fate offers you until you see how it plays out. With the trials he's still to face in Book Four, this is a message he will need to remember, because what he has faced up until now will be as nothing compared with his confrontation with Galbatorix.

The one time that Blagden addresses Eragon specifically is to say the following, "By beak and bone, / Mine blackened stone / Sees rooks and crooks / And bloody brooks!" (*Eldest* p. 545). When Eragon presses him to explain the verse, the raven merely repeats it. Then he teases him by saying, "Son and father alike, both as blind as bats"(*Eldest* p. 546). Needless to say, Eragon, who knows nothing of his parentage at the time, presses Blagden for details about his father. He receives in answer, "While two may share two, / And one of two is certainly one, / One might be two" (*Eldest* p. 546). Although, with the power of hindsight, we can understand — sort of — that the last bit refers to the fact that Eragon's mother gave birth to two children by two separate men, Morzan and Brom, to Eragon, it means absolutely nothing. Despite the fact that he's determined to wrest from the bird the identity of his father, he also thinks that the first bit of verse is of more immediate importance and foretells some sort of impending doom. When he finds out that the Varden expect to be attacked by the Empire at any moment, he naturally assumes that's what Blagden is referring to, especially as it matches his own worry that something momentous is about to happen.

But although Eragon is needed back with the Varden to help them repel the Empire's assault, might there not be more to what Blagden says than just a warning of imminent war? Remember, Blagden is more concerned with fate and destiny than immediate events. Think back to Angela's prophecy of the countless possible futures awaiting Eragon, all of them filled with blood and conflict, but only one bringing happiness and peace, and how he must be careful about losing his way because it will be his own decisions—not somebody else's—that shape his future (*Eragon* p. 204). Now, think of Blagden's verse in terms of that foretelling, and the hidden message behind his repeated cries of "Wyrda," and you have to think there's more to them than just a warning about the Varden being under attack.

There's something that Eragon, like Brom before him, is failing to see in those words, and it has to do with battles. Remember that Angela said that Brom's destiny was to fail at almost everything he attempted, except for killing Morzan (*Eragon* p. 435). Perhaps it was because he could not see beyond what was immediately in front of him. He fought battle after battle, first as a Rider opposing the Forsworn, and then as a member of the Varden in an attempt to overthrow the king. But that approach never worked because he, and the Varden, were not strong enough to defeat Galbatorix and the

Empire in a direct confrontation. The same is true for Eragon; he can barely hold his own against Murtagh and Thorn, even when assisted by Arya and the elvish spellcasters. So how can he hope to survive a direct confrontation with Galbatorix any more than the Varden and their allies can defeat the numerically superior armies of the Empire?

Eragon can't let himself be blinded by the "rooks and crooks / And bloody brooks" (*Eldest* p. 545) of battle, or get caught up in the battles that are sure to ensue between the two sides. He must find another way to both win the war and gain the happiness he deserves. Too many people he loves and cares for, plus all the soldiers serving the Varden, will die in vain if he doesn't find the correct path for himself through the turmoil. It is Eragon's destiny to become the first Dragon Rider since Galbatroix took power to stand against the king and the Empire. In his hands rests the fate of not only his race, but all the people and beings who occupy the lands in which he lives. If he forgets that for a single moment and allows the war to become about him and Galbatorix alone, he will follow in his father's footsteps and fail. Or, even worse, he will end up becoming as self-obsessed as Galbatorix and, instead of overthrowing him, simply replace him.

The latter is, of course, highly unlikely. Eragon is only too aware of that possibility and it terrifies him. Unfortunately, he has already shown that he can be unreasonably stubborn when he doesn't get his own way or doesn't agree with something because he has failed to see the big picture. One need only look at how unreasonable he was when he tried to resist Nasuada's wish to send him as her representative to the dwarves when they were selecting their new king for an example of that (*Brisingr* pp. 364–365). If he persists with that type of blindness, he could make a costly error. In Book Four, he will have to take that next step in maturity. He must heed the hidden message in Blagden's words, realizing that fate does things for a reason and patiently allowing everything to come to fruition before acting. Seeing only what he wants to see, or only what's on the surface, is no longer good enough. In the end, how well he accomplishes that task will determine the outcome of his battle with Galbatorix, not any source of power or newly discovered spell.

Little things, like the pebbles that start an avalanche, sometimes can take on great importance because of what they set in motion or the meanings hidden behind their seemingly insignificant exteriors. Although a person can worry too much, obsessing over every tiny scrap of information that comes their way, the fact remains that some things can't be ignored. In the case of the Inheritance cycle, Paolini has scattered bits of information throughout the first three books that could rain boulders down upon the heads of his characters — or have no bearing on the outcome at all. Eragon will have to sift through everything he's seen and heard, using all the knowledge and resources at his disposal, if he wishes to overcome Galbatorix with as little pain as possible. Obscure, obvious, and everything in between, nothing is small enough to be ignored until it is proven inconsequential, and that is especially true when the lives of people you love are at stake.

Chapter 16

Who Lives? Who Dies?

Starting with the death of Eragon's uncle and Roran's father, Garrow, in the first book of the series, Christopher Paolini has shown that he's not reluctant to kill off major or important characters. Garrow wasn't the only person who didn't make it out of the first book either. Eragon's first teacher, Brom, who is also later revealed to be his father, dies from a wound he incurs at the hands of the Ra'zac (who are also killed, along with their parents, at the beginning of *Brisingr*). And it looks as though we start off *Eldest* with two deaths, when Murtagh vanishes and a group of Urgals, led by the traitorous Twins, kill Nasuada's father, Ajihad, the leader of the Varden (*Eldest* pp. 5–7). It turns out later that Murtagh isn't dead, although some might think that death would have been a better fate than what did happen to him. Murtagh then kills the king of the dwarves, Hrothgar, during the battle of the Burning

Plains (*Eldest* p. 639), so we end up with two deaths among the Varden in *Eldest* anyway.

Of course, the Varden and Eragon aren't the only ones to suffer losses during the first half of the Inheritance cycle. Roran and the villagers of Carvahall suffer more than their fair share of damage while resisting the siege of the Empire's soldiers and the Ra'zac. Yet even though it's not pleasant that Birgit's husband, Quimby, is killed — and eaten — by the Ra'zac, neither his death nor the death of any of the other villagers means quite as much, as they haven't played an important role in the proceedings. But if the deaths of Brom, Ajihad, and Hrothgar were saddening, the ones that hurt the most were those of Oromis and Glaedr. These last two characters were cut down at the end of *Brisingr*. Even though there seemed something inescapable about Oromis's fate, his bravery in the face of his wounds and staring down Galbatorix in the end made his demise all the more heartbreaking (*Brisingr* pp. 734–735).

However, now that there is open war between the Varden and their allies and the Empire, we're going to have to be prepared to suffer more losses over the course of Book Four.

Even worse is the fact that there's a darn good chance that people we've grown to like over the course of the series will be among the fallen. None of us can say for sure what Paolini is going to do in Book Four, but I think that we can safely say that Eragon and Saphira will live while Galbatorix and Shruikan will die. Of course, in the case of the last, there's always the chance that with the death of the king, Shruikan will be freed of the enchantments he was under that forced him to serve the king. Hopefully, not being subject to the same ties that connect other Riders to their dragons, he won't feel the despair that a dragon normally suffers when his or her Rider dies and will retain the will to live. However, death might be a mercy for him, as he's supposedly been driven insane by being forced to fly for Galbatorix. It's nice to think that the death of the king could liberate him, and he can go back to being a free dragon, but that's probably wishful thinking.

As far as the rest of the characters in the series go, whether they live or die might seem a matter of your guess being as good as mine. However, by looking at each of them, the role they play in the series, and the effect their death would have on the fate of others, it should be possible to determine their chances of survival on a scale of 1 to 100—with 0 being dead as a doornail and 100 meaning coming through without a scratch. Aside from Eragon, Saphira, and the king, nobody else is going to come up with either full marks or 0 next to their name, but some of them are as good as dead while others look to be in for smooth sailing—at least if the rest of the predictions in this book work out. As unfortunate as it sounds, for some to live, prosper, and fulfill their destiny, others will have to die, whether we like it or not. So as Blagden the raven says before every one of his pronouncements, "Wyrda"—Fate!

(The names are in alphabetical order, so the sequence has no bearing on their chances of survival. Beside each name is the number representing the chances of them making it through to the end of Book Four and beyond. Remember, the higher the number, the higher the chances of their survival. Each name is accompanied by the reasons for their rating, substantiated as much as possible from the story.)

ANGELA   80

Angela has been around long enough to remember the Forsworn, and seems to know everything that goes on in Alagaësia and the surrounding countries. Everyone from the elves to the dwarves at least knows of her. Even Oromis recounts a visit she once made to Ellesméra, and calls her an "extraordinary person" (*Brisingr* p. 639). As we get to know her throughout the course of the series, we find out that she's not only a fortuneteller of some skill, but also an herbalist, a spellcaster, and a fierce warrior, capable of defeating warriors twice her size in battle. Yet, even though these attributes have all stood her in good stead over the years, she is most liable to survive mainly because of her intelligence. One can have all the power in the world and still be killed easily in battle or by another magic user if you don't have the brains to know what to do with your abilities, and of all the people Eragon has met, she's the least liable to end up doing something stupid that will get her killed.

One gets the sense that Angela is a survivor, and no matter how dire a situation might be, she will always find a way out of it. It's hard to imagine her panicking no matter what's happening, or her ingenuity failing her when she needs it most. If worse came to worse, she could probably talk her opponents to death, or at least have them so baffled and confused she'd have time to slip away while they were trying to figure out if she had insulted them or not.

Although anybody can be struck down by a wayward arrow during a battle—and she doesn't shrink from fighting, so that chance is always there—she'll survive, if only because she's so much fun to have around. There are certain characters you just know an author won't kill off because of what they bring to a story, and the amount of fun the author appears to have had writing about them. Paolini has gone to a lot of effort with Angela, and I can't help feeling he enjoys thinking up the diatribes and insults that she comes out with. I don't see him depriving himself of the fun she provides—who else would there be to give everyone a hard time and to keep them on their toes—by killing her off at any time in Book Four. After all, Angela has to survive the war, and the series, for, as she'd be the first to tell you, somebody is going to have to keep Eragon in line!

ARYA   80

A lot of people will figure that Arya has to survive because she and Eragon are destined to be with each other, or at least because the last dragon egg will hatch for her. But the truth is more prosaic. The reason she needs to survive is so that she can become queen of the elves when her mother is killed in battle. Under normal circumstances, she might have refused to succeed her mother, for even as we find out that she is heir to the throne on Eragon's first visit to Dur Weldenvarden, we also find out that she has mixed feelings about this (*Eldest* p. 309). Yet in time of war, when continuity in leadership is vital, she would have no choice but to step into the breech left by her mother's death. As she herself said, when explaining to Eragon why she risked her life as both ambassador to the Varden and courier of Saphira's egg even though she was the sole heir to the throne,

"To us, a king or queen's highest responsibility is to serve their people however and whenever possible. If that means forfeiting our life in the process, we welcome the opportunity to prove our devotion to – as the dwarves say – hearth, hall, and honor." (Eldest p. 309)

Well, what greater way to prove her devotion to the elvish people than to ascend to the throne and lead their armies in what the elves see as a war to redeem themselves after allowing Galbatorix to overthrow the original Dragon Riders?

So Arya has to live to succeed her mother as queen, and if, as is to be hoped, Galbatorix is overthrown, to lead the elves into the new world. No one is better suited to do that than she is, for she is the only elf to have had regular contact with the three other races over the past seventy years, the only one with sufficient knowledge of the other races to deal with them successfully. For if the elves want a say in how the world works, they will have to be involved in it and have a leader who can communicate with the other leaders.

BIRGIT 30

Birgit played a key role in ensuring the townspeople of Carvahall made the journey across Alagaësia from their village to the country of Surda and to the relative safety offered by the Varden. She was driven by her desire for vengeance against the Ra'zac and the king because of the death of her husband during the siege of Carvahall. However, she has also sworn an oath against Roran that he will be forced to compensate her and her family, because if it hadn't been for him, the Ra'zac and the Empire's soldiers would never have attacked their village. She swore to see that oath fulfilled once the Ra'zac had been dealt with and they were all safe (*Brisingr* p. 156).

Yet, as was mentioned earlier, she seems to have softened somewhat in her stance, even standing up for Katrina when she and Roran were married. The problem is that an oath is an oath. She's bound by what she swore. The only way that she could possibly be free of it would be to die. I think it would give her great satisfaction to die saving either Roran's or Katrina's life, leaving him forever in her debt. She will exact her payment from Roran through making him give her family and herself the land he inherited from his father, Garrow. There's no way that he would be able to refuse her if she made a deathbed request after having just saved either him or Katrina.

BLÖDHGARM   50

As the leader of the twelve spellcasters assigned by Queen Islanzadí as Eragon's personal magical bodyguards, Blödhgarm is especially at risk when Eragon is in battle. He and the other elves must link their minds to Eragon's magically so that Eragon can draw upon their energy during a fight. Despite the fact that Blödhgarm is a powerful being — and an enigmatic figure as well, seeing as how he is covered in fur — he is also incredibly vulnerable when linked to Eragon. Like all the elves, he is probably willing to sacrifice himself in order for Eragon to stay alive. In the event of an all-out attack upon Eragon, Blödhgarm would probably let himself be drained dry if it meant that Eragon lived to fight another day. I have an awful feeling that Eragon might let his pride get in the way of his common sense and directly challenge Galbatorix at some point. He will escape only because Blödhgarm and others give their lives in order to protect him.

Hopefully, Eragon will be more considerate than that, recalling that other lives are on the line and remembering that he doesn't stand a chance in a direct confrontation with the king unless Galbatorix is cut off from the source of his power. Even if Eragon is considerate of his magical bodyguards, chances aren't great that Blödhgarm will make it anyway, for he's one of Eragon's physical bodyguards as well, which means that he is prepared to throw himself in front of any arrow or sword that's heading toward Eragon. Mortality rates among bodyguards of those who fight on the front lines aren't the best under normal circumstance. When your charge is a reckless seventeen-year-old who is the focus of the entire Empire's enmity, your chances are even less.

ELVA 70

There was a time when Elva might have welcomed death as a relief from the torments she suffered as a result of Eragon's misguided blessing. Now that he's been able to partially reverse the spell, giving her a semblance of control over herself, she wouldn't welcome it. In fact, she seems to be looking forward to taking advantage of her powers, using them to whatever advantage they give her. Due to her ability to manipulate people by knowing their deepest fears and emotions, she has little to fear from anybody when it comes to a direct confrontation. Being still only the size of a small child, and just over a year old, the chances of her being in battle are slim, especially because she is no longer serving as a personal adviser to Nasuada (*Brisingr* p. 268). This reduces her chances of being killed by accident to about the same as any other civilian. However, she is still a being of power. And power has a nasty tendency to attract power, which means she could come to the attention of an enemy magic user and face attack in that manner.

But the fact that Angela has sworn to keep an eye on her "for the next decade" (*Brisingr* p. 270) means that she is also being protected by a very powerful being, and it would be hard to get past her defenses. There's also the fact that she carries the mark of the dragons on her forehead, placed there by Saphira as her part in blessing Elva. Although nobody is sure of its significance—not even Oromis could explain it—there's always the chance that it means she's destined to become a Dragon Rider. After all, only Riders have ever borne that mark, so why shouldn't it be an omen of what's to approach for her? By the time that Elva is old enough, it's possible that Saphira's first clutch of eggs will be ready to choose their Riders. Fate has important things in store for Elva, and I don't think that death at the hands of Galbatorix or his soldiers will have anything to do with it.

(The next two in alphabetical order are Eragon and Galbatorix, and we'll save them for a separate chapter, although the former is 100 and the latter 0.)

HELEN AND JEOD   60

Now that Helen has the means to regain the fortune that was stolen from them when Galbatorix ruined their business because Jeod was supplying the Varden, she has plenty to live for. As a noncombatant, she won't be seeing any direct action, so she has a better chance of survival than someone serving on the front lines. However, by setting herself up as a merchant who will be trading with the Varden and their allies, she's more at risk than if she were a stay-at-home housewife. Remember, the king has made a practice of targeting merchants and traders who deal with his enemies, so Helen will have to be careful and discreet in her business dealings. She seems to be smart enough, and have sufficient sense, to not only realize that, but to figure out the best way to carry on her business so that she stays as safe as possible. The only thing that could potentially cause her problems is her ambition and desire to make money. These passions could overwhelm her common sense and lead her to take a dangerous risk that results in disaster.

Therefore, although Helen will most likely survive the war and the series, she'll have to be careful and smart to do so. However, greed and ambition can do strange things to people, and occasionally blind them to reality. Helen she spent a long time "suffering" the indignity of a reduced status, so she might not be as careful as she should, in an effort to regain her lost standing. Chances are, she'll be fine; but with the job she's taken on, nothing is 100 percent guaranteed.

Although Jeod claims that his standing among the Varden is no higher than that of a swordsman, that's probably not true, for he has skills and knowledge far beyond that of the average soldier. Combine that with his advanced years, and he's not liable to see much in the way of battle. For Nasuada has proven herself to be an astute leader, and is unlikely to waste a man of his talents on the battlefield, when he could be put to far better use. Instead of fighting, he could be researching documents for clues as to the whereabouts of more secret tunnels into the king's palace, or the location of the Vault of Souls, which we know to be a key to overthrowing Galbatorix. The other reason that Jeod is likely to survive is that he would be an ideal person to help take over the governing of Alagaësia when the battle's over, as he is well versed in the history of the country. At the very least, Jeod would make an excellent adviser to whomever assumes the mantle of leadership, for he has the knowledge to help reestablish all the branches of government that Galbatorix destroyed during his reign. With the death of Brom, Jeod is the one human with a significant knowledge of the past, and he will have a key role to play in the future of Alagaësia.

QUEEN ISLANDÍ   25

See Arya.

MURTAGH   30

It would be nice to think that Murtagh will survive and be redeemed through some heroic action, but even if he were to survive the war, too many people would be demanding that he pay for what he did while fighting for Galbatorix. Not only did he kill Hrothgar, king of the dwarves, but it was his sword that killed Oromis. Eragon tried to reduce the popular perception of Murtagh's responsibility for that act by saying that Galbatorix used Murtagh and Thorn to kill Oromis and Glaedr. Nonetheless, they still did it. Anyway, in spite of what Eragon might say, Murtagh hasn't been without blame, as he turned his back on Eragon's offer of help to break free of the king by refusing to contemplate changing his nature. The anger and resentment that Murtagh feels toward the world for the way his life has turned out have trapped him in a web that he can't escape. With each bad thing that happens to him, those bonds only grip him tighter. Killing Oromis and Glaedr was probably the last straw; he probably can't decide whom he hates more—himself or the world.

The best that Murtagh can hope for is to find a measure of redemption by dying while protecting Eragon somehow from the king. There can't be any heroic comeback for him and Thorn, as they are too far steeped in blood to come back to the side of the angels. But Murtagh might gain inner peace before he dies by protecting his younger brother from Galbatorix. Hopefully, his death will also give Eragon a chance to free the Eldunarí that Murtagh has been using.

NASUADA 80

Nasuada stands out pretty obviously and makes an easy target when she rides into battle. But she is so well protected by her bodyguard that there is little chance of her coming to harm during any of the battles that the Varden will face in their quest to overthrow the Empire. Anyway, having already had her survive assassination attempts and the Trial of the Long Knives—plus killing her father in *Eldest*—the chances of Paolini killing her off now are minimal. Anyway, there's a good chance that she will not only hook up with Eragon but will have the last dragon egg hatch for her. She and Eragon will retire to the relative peace of Du Weldenvarden, where he will train the next generation of Dragon Riders, and she'll be his first pupil and wife.

ORIK, king of the dwarves   70

Although there are no guarantees when it comes to a warrior surviving a battle—especially a dwarf king who leads his troops into the thick of things—Eragon and Nasuada's clan brother, Orik, should come out of this alive. In fact, the worst threat he faces isn't from Galbatorix's forces, but from the rebel clans within his own fold, especially Az Sweldn rak Anhûin. This clan tried to assassinate Eragon during the meetings when he was elected king. Despite the fact that they are now shunned by the other clans—treated as though they no longer exist—it doesn't mean that they can't and won't cause damage. It's their presence lurking in the background that lowers his chances of survival to only 70 percent, but I don't think we're liable to see a second dwarf king die. The series is going to need a dwarf king who is used to dealing with the outside world. As with Arya leading the elves, there isn't anybody more suited to the job of leading the dwarves than Orik.

ORRIN, king of Surda   50

Orrin is expendable in that there will probably be no place for an independent Surda in the new kingdom of Alagaësia. After the war is over, a new way of governing will have to be figured out. In other words, Paolini can kill him off without any major repercussions and help make it easier to solve the problem of who is to rule the humans in the new country. Orrin is a nice guy, but you get the feeling that he's slightly ineffectual and somewhat insecure, not a great combination when it comes to leading a new country. Instead of seeing him cast aside after the war, it would be better for him to die in the final battle. Of course, if he does survive, he could devote himself to his experiments and be perfectly content living out the rest of his days in that way, although he could still end up dying in a laboratory accident if he's not careful. Still, don't look for him to live to see the end of the war.

RORAN AND KATRINA   80

Ever since Roran convinced the villagers of Carvahall to pack up and move to Surda so that he could rescue Katrina, the fates of Roran and Katrina have been irrevocably intertwined. With the added protection that Eragon has offered both of them—they can summon either himself or Saphira if they are ever in need—plus the wards he's placed on Roran to protect him in battle, they have a better chance of surviving the war than most. Although Galbatorix might try to get at Roran again by attacking Katrina, he's already seen how that plan can backfire. The first time he attempted it, four of his most powerful servants—the Ra'zac and their parents—died (*Brisingr* pp. 36–66). Having killed off both Brom and Garrow, and with Murtagh unlikely to survive the war, it's highly unlikely that Paolini will leave Eragon completely bereft of family by killing off Roran. And as long as he's able to draw breath, there's no chance that Roran is going to let anything happen to Katrina.

Both Roran and Katrina will live out their natural life span, but probably not in the way they had foreseen when they first talked of marrying, because it's doubtful that they will end up as farmers. Although Roran might not have a dragon in his future, he will be a figure of power and authority in the new world. He will be seeing plenty of both his cousin and all the others he fought with in the Varden, as only befits one of the human rulers of the new land.

It may seem that I'm overly optimistic in my predictions about who will live and who will die, as I predict that only two characters won't make it through to the end of the series. However, if you look at the first three books, and how the major characters have fared, you'll realize that, although Paolini hasn't been reluctant to kill them off, he hasn't made a habit of it either. Although they haven't been in a state of open warfare until now, they have all consistently faced danger since *Eragon*, and only three of them have died in that time. Perhaps I'm being too hopeful in my outlook, but I just can't see any way of justifying killing off any characters other than the ones I have named.

Chapter 17

Eragon and Galbatorix, and How It All Ends

In the course of this analysis of Christopher Paolini's Inheritance cycle, we've looked at the various ways available to Eragon for defeating Galbatorix and tried to see what the world will look like once the battle is over. Although Paolini has offered us some fairly definite clues as to what and who are going to be important before the dust settles, there are still enough gaps in our knowledge that we can't be sure just how it will all be resolved. For instance, although the mystery of how Galbatorix has been able to augment his powers to such a great extent has been explained through Oromis and Glaedr's explanation of the Eldunarí, the dragon's heart of hearts (*Brisingr* pp. 627–637), only the most obscure of clues have been offered as to how he can be overcome.

For aside from Solembum's cryptic pronouncement regarding the Rock of Kuthian and the Vault of Souls (*Eragon* p. 206), nobody has offered Eragon even a hint about how to overcome the king. Of course, finding the Vault of Souls looks to be as major a quest as anything that Eragon has attempted at any point in the series; hardly anyone has even heard of the Rock of Kuthian, let alone knows where it and the Vault of Souls might lie. What makes this especially frustrating is the fact that Solembum has already proven to be a reliable source of information, for it was he who set Eragon on the correct trail for obtaining his new sword.

Maybe the vault has something to do with either the Eldunarí or the spirits who inhabit Alagaësia. Although everything in the story suggests otherwise, Oromis was convinced that all the hearts of hearts were accounted for. So there is still the chance that this repository existed from the days prior to the alliance of the dragons and the elves. The elves think that the dragons gave all the Eldunarí in existence to the Riders for safekeeping, but maybe the dragons held some back out of mistrust. The other possibility is that the spirits are what remains of the mysterious Grey Folk, who exhausted themselves casting the spell that turned the ancient language into the means of controlling magic, and that the Vault of Souls is the means to communicate with them directly.

Of course, all of this is guesswork. Paolini has been incredibly reticent when it comes to supplying information about what it will take to defeat the king or about the Vault of Souls. All we know is that whatever happens, they will be key in the quest to overthrow Galbatorix. However, no matter how much power Eragon amasses and no matter how successful he is in reducing the king's power by separating him from his source of Eldunarí, he will still be at a decided disadvantage in any confrontation with the king. Galbatorix has had centuries to hone his skills and practice his art, compared with Eragon's couple of years. You can also bet that, like other magic users we've met, he's spent the time squirreling away energy, so he can draw upon it in times of need. If Eragon has the ring, Aren, in which Brom stashed energy and the belt of Beloth the Wise (*Eldest* p. 554), in whose twelve diamonds he can stockpile energy, think of the equivalents that Galbatorix might have. Even with the backing of his twelve elven spellcasters and Glaedr's Eldunarí, Eragon is still going to be hard pressed to match the king.

Think back to the message that Brom "recorded" with Saphira for Eragon, the advice and warnings he gives him concerning a confrontation with Galbatorix. The first thing he says is to remember that in a wizards' duel, intelligence is much more important than strength. In order to defeat an opponent, a spellcaster has to figure out how that opponent interprets information and reacts to the world. Only then will you know their weaknesses and be able to strike effectively. Battering blindly at someone's mind won't accomplish anything, as Eragon has discovered in all of his battles with Murtagh. The object is to find a spell that is able to slip through an enemy's defenses. The second part of Brom's advice follows a similar line, as he warns Eragon not to fixate on one idea alone; he must always be thinking and trying different things in an attempt to find the gaps in Galbatorix's reasoning. Although the king is insane—which makes it difficult to predict what he will do and think—it also means that there are things he won't think of defending himself against but that an ordinary person would take for granted (*Brisingr* pp. 623–624).

Despite the fact that the knowledge of Galbatorix's true name is not something that can be used in battle against him, because of the warding spells he's cast that will kill anyone trying to utter it, knowledge of his true nature could be a key to overcoming him. Eragon needs to spend a great deal of time and energy on this task if he wants to understand how the king thinks and where any gaps in his reasoning might be. If he fixates only on discovering how to sever Galbatorix's connection to the Eldunarí, he'll not be fully prepared when he finally does confront him. Unfortunately, there would be a cost for this carelessness, probably in the form of other people dying in order for him to stay alive.

In some ways, Eragon remains his own worst enemy. Yes, he has proven himself an able and adept pupil, learning most of what Brom and Oromis had to teach him quickly. And he has been magically augmented, so that he is now almost the physical equal of an elf. But he has yet to overcome those flaws in his own character that have proven to be stumbling blocks to his emotional maturity. He is still almost mulish in his stubbornness, which means that he is blinkered to another person's point of view. Anytime he has had to surrender his own position in favor of someone else's, he's done so only grudgingly. If you want an example of his tendency to fixate, look no further than his relationship with Arya. He absolutely refuses to understand that she has no interest in him romantically.

As a result, he continually risks alienating her as a friend by insisting on pursuing the matter, even after she has made it perfectly clear how inappropriate this is.

For Eragon to defeat Galbatorix, he will also, in a sense, have to defeat himself. He will have to delve deep inside and examine himself with all the objectivity he can muster. He can't be afraid to realize his own shortcomings and what he has to do in order to overcome them. During Eragon's final visit to Du Weldenvarden, Oromis asks him what spell he would most like to learn, and he asks to be taught his true name. Oromis denies his request, telling him that doing so would mean that he would gain some profit from knowing it, but wouldn't obtain any of the wisdom he would gain by taking that journey to self-awareness on his own (*Brisingr* pp. 641–642). There's no point in Eragon knowing his true name if he doesn't understand what it is about himself that makes that name significant. If he can examine his life and his relationships with the same dispassion that he brought to his examination of Sloan's character (*Brisingr* pp. 79–80), which revealed to him the butcher's true name, he will not only find out his own true name, he will be far better prepared for fighting Galbatorix. Although there's a lot of truth in the saying, "Know your enemy," in this case, it's just as important for Eragon to know himself.

Although there is no doubt in any reader's mind that Eragon and Saphira will triumph over Galbatorix in the end, the means that they will use to accomplish this are still hidden. However, it will most likely take a combination of a few things, not the least of which is Eragon's own determination to succeed and his desire to keep the people he loves safe at all costs. At the end of *Brisingr*, as he and Saphira look out over the city of Feinster, which the Varden have just conquered, they are united in their resolve to do what they must in order to overcome Galbatorix. And Eragon greets the rising sun, anticipating the battles to come and victory over the king (*Brisingr* p. 748).

In response to his earlier query, "What now?" Nasuada responded, "We will march north to Belatona, and when we have captured it, we will proceed onward…[and] cast down Galbatorix or die trying" (*Brisingr* p. 746). But as far as Eragon is concerned, there is nothing conditional about their task — they cannot, they will not fail. That's the sort of determination that finds a way to win, no matter how difficult or trying it might prove.

Of course, the story won't end with the death of Galbatorix and the defeat of his armies. Of primary concern for all will be the establishment of a new government and restoring the Dragon Riders to their former glory. With Arya established as queen of the elves and with Orik king of the dwarves, the human kingdom is the one where there will be a real vacuum in leadership. The issue of what's to become of the Urgals will also need to be settled. This warlike race will have to learn to change their ways, so that they can coexist with their neighbors peacefully.

Therefore, it will be necessary for the humans to have a strong leader, one whom the Urgals will respect. However, it can't be a warlord. It will have to be someone with an understanding of what the common people have to deal with, so that he or she can win their support and unite what is sure to be a divided population. Remember, they have just fought what amounts to a civil war, and there's bound to be recrimination and resentment on both sides.

Nasuada would be the ideal person to lead the Varden, except that the majority of Alagaësia would not be able to identify with her for a variety of reason, not the least of which is her heritage. Besides, she's liable to be busy with other matters and not willing to take up the reins of power. Eragon has already said that he has no interest in ruling (*Eragon* p. 443). He'd rather fulfill the obligations of the Dragon Riders of old, ensuring that all are treated fairly. And anyway, he's going to have his hands full training future Riders. No, when it comes down to it, there's going to be only one person suited for assuming the responsibility of first ruler of the human population after the fall of Galbatorix: Roran.

Aside from the fact that he has proven himself able to lead people simply on the power of his convictions — we saw him convince the people of Carvahall to travel across the country — he's also a respected, and more than a little feared, warrior who has earned the respect of the Urgals. Of course, it doesn't hurt that he is Eragon's cousin and is able to call upon either him or Saphira at a moment's notice. Roran is also intelligent enough to know that he doesn't know everything, and will seek out those with wisdom to be his advisers. First among those will be Jeod, whom he came to know and trust during the villagers' escape to Surda.

This will have the bonus for Jeod of making his wife, Helen, especially happy, as he will finally obtain the status she thinks he deserves. Of course, as she's by this time well on the way to becoming a highly successful businessperson, she's probably less concerned about matters of that sort these days. With his knowledge of history, Jeod will be invaluable for the advice he can offer in helping to establish the type of government that will best suit the new country and teaching Roran the ins and outs of running the country.

There will be problems, of course, what with people getting used to sharing the land with Urgals and with others attempting to settle scores with those who served under Galbatorix, but that's what the Dragon Rider is for: to make sure that all is well for all the people and to keep the peace among them. It's not going to be easy for the people of Alagaësia or their neighbors, but it's going to be a darn sight better than it ever was in the days of the Empire. The days of the Dragon Riders are returning, and that will be an excellent thing.

Afterword

Over the course of writing *What Will Happen in Eragon IV*, the hardest task I faced was not becoming wrapped up in the story. You see, periodically I'd have to refer back to one of the three books already published to check a fact or a quote, and all of a sudden I'd find that I'd sat and read a hundred pages without noticing. The world that Christopher Paolini has created with his Inheritance cycle is so compelling that it's almost impossible not to become caught up in it. It doesn't matter if it's the first page of *Eragon* or the middle of *Eldest*; once you start reading, you don't want to stop.

The second-hardest task I faced was separating out what I wanted to happen in the story from what I thought actually would happen. Like all fans of the books, I've got my favorite characters and my favorite moments, and would dearly love to see certain things happen. However, I was writing a book that predicted what would happen in Book Four of the Inheritance cycle, not what I wanted to happen. That meant that I couldn't just look for proof to substantiate my likes and dislikes, but had to consider everything that Paolini had to offer on a given subject.

I know that there are predictions in this book that people will disagree with. I also know that there will be questions raised as to why I didn't talk about such and such or so-and-so. That's fine. I can live with that. I knew when I began writing this book that I was wading into dangerous waters. Those who are going to care enough about the fate of Eragon and Saphira to read this book are also going to be those who are truly passionate about the series and its characters. You are the people who are going to have the strongest and most fiercely held opinions on what's going to happen and why.

However, as far as I'm concerned, there's only one person who knows what's going to happen, and that's the author — Christopher Paolini. I would never presume to say that what I've offered here in this book are anything more than educated, well-thought-out guesses. In the end, that's all any of us can really do when trying to predict what someone else is going to write. I've done my best to substantiate my predictions through references to the story. Still, the book is only my interpretation of events and their implications for the future. Someone else could easily read the same sentence that I did, decide that it meant something else altogether, and come up with a totally different prediction as to what's going to happen.

Afterword

I wrote this book in the hope that people would have fun reading my predictions and deciding whether they agreed with them. Also, I wrote it as a way of encouraging people to delve beneath the surface of the story and come to a deeper appreciation of just what Paolini has accomplished with the creation of the Inheritance cycle. Although overanalyzing a book can ruin it, that doesn't mean that there can't be some benefits derived from reading between the lines and trying to figure out any deeper meanings that the author has tried to impart to the reader.

I like to encourage people to think. So even if you disagree with everything I say or predict in this book, I'll still consider it a success because you thought about the book and came up with your own conclusions. I hope that you had a good time wandering through Alagaësia with me and exploring the fantastic world that the author has created for our enjoyment. And I can't wait to hear what *you* think might happen in Book Four. I had a lot of fun writing this book, but I have a feeling that the fun is only just beginning, now that you've read it and want to have your say.

Other Ulysses Press Titles

Mugglenet.com's Harry Potter Should Have Died: Controversial Views from the #1 Fan Site

Emerson Spartz and Ben Schoen, $14.95

This book brings the original and entertaining views of the experts behind Mugglenet.com to 100 of the most interesting and contentious debate topics in the Potter world.

The Unofficial Harry Potter Vocabulary Builder: Learn the 3,000 Hardest Words from All Seven Books and Enjoy the Series More

Sayre Van Young, $16.95

This book is a complete and helpful reference that provides young readers with the perfect tool for increasing their knowledge of words while allowing them to more fully enjoy the best-selling kids' series of all time.

The Zombie Handbook: How to Identify the Living Dead and Survive the Coming Zombie Apocalypse

Rob Sacchetto, $16.95

This book reveals the vital information that [human] readers need to know about identifying, understanding and, when things get ugly, dispatching the "living dead."

To order these books call 800-377-2542 or 510-601-8301, fax 510-601-8307, e-mail ulysses@ulyssespress.com, or write to Ulysses Press, P.O. Box 3440, Berkeley, CA 94703. All retail orders are shipped free of charge. California residents must include sales tax. Allow two to three weeks for delivery.

About the Author

Richard Marcus is an accomplished book and music critic whose work has appeared both online and in printed publications around the world in various languages. He has been featured in the German edition of *Rolling Stone Magazine* and in *The Bangladesh Star*; he wrote the liner notes for Eagle Rock Entertainment's DVD "Willy DeVille Live at Montreux 1994"; and he has been quoted on dust jackets and in artist's publicity materials. Online he is editor of the South East Asian arts and culture magazine *Epic India Magazine*, is a contributing editor for the web-magazine Blogcritics.org, is a freelance contributor to the German-based quadrilingual (English, German, Turkish, and Arabic) maga-